# Sebastian
### and the
# GO-KART
# GIRL

## JONATHAN DAY

ARTISTS GATE
PRESS

*To Pamala Thomas Ward*

"New York is always hopeful. Always it believes that something good is about to come off, and it must hurry to meet it."

–Dorothy Parker

# CHAPTER 1

**"IT'S TIME,"** my dad says.

I look up from my computer screen in what Dad calls his Innovation Factory, where my sister and I are working this summer.

"Go get 'em!" he urges.

The "'em" would be the other contestants in the New York State Regional Teen Math Olympics.

"I accidentally nailed my feet to the floor, so I can't go right now," I tell him.

"You're mentally superior, Sebastian. Don't let your shyness stop you."

Mentally quick enough to be scared, that is.

Dad takes me by the arm and gently escorts me to the door. "I know you'll kick butt."

Is there doubt in his voice, or do I just hear it?

My sister, Lilly, punches my shoulder softly two times. Even though she's only four years older than me, she's wiser than most grown-ups, and her punches are her way of expressing confidence in me. I wish I had confidence in me.

My parents think I can sometimes get lost in my thoughts, so they made sure I have a brilliant app on my phone to show me what subway train to take and when to get off.

I'm practicing answering math problems on my phone when I realize the 1 train has stopped at the Chambers Street station, where I have to get off. I jump between the doors just before they slide closed.

Stuyvesant is a very competitive public high school where the Math Olympics will take place. I cross over a highway on the pedestrian bridge to get there, along with other kids my age.

Some of them are skinny-tall. Some are short like me. They look like they've come from all over the world: there are kids with turbans, Middle Eastern kids, Asian kids, Black kids, and pale kids like me. Brains have no skin color, as my dad likes to say.

They all go right through the school entrance like there's no danger of failure or humiliation in there. I hesitate. My palms are sweaty. I'm having a little trouble breathing, and I feel dizzy.

Okay. It's time.

*I slouch into the auditorium, get my competitor's number, and wait until I hear my name: Sebastian Kemp. I climb onto the stage. Three judges sit at a table near the front row of seats.*

*The judge tapping a pencil on a grading sheet is eager to record my wrong answers. The man with Einstein-wild white hair has glacier-cold blue eyes. Cold enough to freeze my brain cells? The woman has lots of very white not-smiling teeth, which she bares like a threatening dog.*

Competitors fill the seats behind them. Their glasses magnify their eyes, so all I see is an angry army of eyeballs eager for me to fail.

I hear a voice, but the words are unclear because of the nervous buzzing in my ears.

"I will repeat the question only once," Einstein threatens. "What is the square root of one thousand three hundred and sixty-nine?"

Easy: thirty-seven. But no words come out, only mouse squeaks.

"Ten seconds to answer," Bright Teeth growls.

I shout out, "Thirty-seven!" but apparently only in my head, because Tap-Tap-Tap keeps tapping out the seconds.

I pant for breath. I'm not dead, but I wish I were.

This is what could happen if I actually go into the auditorium. So I don't. I don't go get 'em.

Dad will be 100 percent disappointed in me. I don't go back to the Innovation Factory, where we work and where he lives now that he and Mom are separated. Instead, I head home to our apartment near the Museum of Natural History on the Upper West Side of Manhattan. My mood improves just a little because I spot a hawk soaring free and fretless on a breeze while I'm walking from the subway to our building. But as it flies lower, I realize it's just a mangy seagull. I guess I don't deserve to see a hawk today.

# CHAPTER 2

**MOM'S PREPARING LESSON PLANS** at the dining room table, which doubles as her office. She's the head of the science department at Tarbell on the East Side, and she also teaches biology. I'd love to be in her class, but the school 'is just for girls.

"You're home early," she says, a little puzzled.

Which would be worse—to tell her that I lost because I wasn't smart enough or that I didn't even go inside the building because I was too nervous? Maybe I could say a gazillion locusts descended on the school, and it was unsafe to even approach it. But she knows I like to add spice to stories to make them more exciting or dramatic. She wouldn't believe that for a nanosecond.

I go into my room, where our dog, Lucky, is asleep on my bed. He's a stray my sister and I found in Central Park and adopted. I sit next to him, and he puts his head on my lap because he always knows when I'm sad.

Mom comes in and perches on the edge of the bed too. "Can I ask you something?"

She already has. "I guess."

"Did you win?"

I shake my head. "I couldn't go inside."

She gives me a hug. I wish she wouldn't be so understanding about my failings.

"Being shy isn't a curse, and it doesn't mean you're a bad person, Sebastian. The anxiety you feel about the competition is like asthma or allergies. There are ways to treat it."

"You mean go back to Dr. Pry and Poke, who poked me with questions. Talking about it just made me shyer."

She smiles sadly and leaves my room.

I can talk easily with my friend Luke, so I video chat with him on my computer. "Do you think being shy is a disease?" I ask.

"I really don't know. I'll have to look it up."

Luke is excellent at finding out stuff on the internet. "How about watching *The Big Bang Theory*?" he asks. That's a TV show about a group of scientist friends. They're brilliant but maybe a little awkward around girls and stuff.

Luke and I stream "The Dumpling Paradox" from the first season, and it does cheer me up enough that I actually laugh. There's a knock on my door, and Mom sticks her head in.

"I love it when I hear you laughing," she says in her happy voice.

"This is a superior episode."

"I heard two laughs."

"Luke's watching on his computer. We have a chat set up, so it might sound like he's in my room, but he's on speaker."

"Luke?"

"From school. He's not with us anymore, though."

"You make it sound like he moved to another planet."

"New Jersey."

"Hmmm."

# CHAPTER 3

**MY SISTER GETS** *hmmm*ed about zero times.

I know my parents have secretly trained her to herd me around the city like a sheep that needs protection. Every morning, she and I take the subway to the Queensboro Plaza station across the East River in Queens, then walk to work. I usually have to half-run to keep up because she strides so fast and is 97 percent as graceful as an impala. Today, the shepherd's walking at my pace.

"He signed you up, didn't he?" The *he* is our dad.

"Yeah."

"If the Math Olympics had been your thing, you would have conquered it."

I don't know. Maybe. Lilly's an okay older sister, but she'd be a lot better if she had a flaw. Or seven.

The Innovation Factory is in an old warehouse.

Lilly is working with Dad to build a neat solar-powered delivery van. I'm writing computer code to help his colleague Harold create a video game.

Dad and Lilly's work area takes up the most space because of all the tools, the hundreds of parts bins, the computers, and the 3D printer that's as big as a small car. When we arrive, Lilly immediately starts sorting out a tangle of electrical wires attached to the van's dashboard.

I go to my shiny metal-and-glass desk with three computer screens in the video game area. Whiteboards covered with diagrams and flow charts outlining how the game develops are hanging on the wall. Harold has a similar computer setup, luckily not too close to mine. Sometimes he doesn't shower and can kinda smell.

Next to us inside the warehouse is an entire house with a roof, modeled on an Amish farmhouse Dad saw in Pennsylvania. He loved the building's proportions and the door and window placement and thought it was the most perfect home he had ever seen. He wanted an exact copy, so he brought Amish carpenters here to build it.

Dad's a computer engineer who admires farmers who don't use motors, computers, or power tools. Mom calls this ironic. She often uses words my sister and I don't know, and we're required to look up their meanings.

My dad comes to his house door and waves me in. "Pancakes!"

He used to be in charge of breakfast on Sunday mornings when our family was still together. While he cooked, I'd usually describe one of my fantastic dreams. Now he only makes pancakes when he wants to have a serious talk. Mom must have texted him about my Olympic failure.

We sit at his wooden-plank dining room table, but I don't eat because my stomach gets upset when I'm upset. Dad isn't eating either. His stomach must be churning too.

"You spend a lot of time alone in front of your computer, don't you, Sebastian?"

"I guess I do."

"It's summertime. Get out of your room. Clear your brain with some fresh air. Isn't there a chess club or something for teenagers at the outdoor chess tables in Central Park? You can find guys who share your talents and interests. You can make a friend."

This is something my sister would do with no worries. She's about as shy as a firecracker.

"Can I help?" my dad asks.

I don't know. He doesn't either.

Back at my desk, I search the internet to see if there is a club for teens at the Chess & Checkers House, but I don't find one. The house is on a hill in Central Park, and I used to take chess lessons from our neighbor Mr. B before he died. He was very nice, and I miss him. He challenged me to play at a more advanced level, and one time he gave me an old subway token. I still don't know if it had magic in it, but I beat the best chess player in school with the token hanging around my neck on a chain. I wish I'd had it when I went to the Math Olympics.

The doorbell interrupts my daydreaming about Mr. B and the token. On the security camera, there's a teenage girl who looks as sleek as a Doberman. She's about Lilly's age, and when I buzz the lock, she bounds in, and I realize she's Kyle Ryan's daughter, Naomi.

"Sebastian!" she yells.

Her bright red sneakers with prancing black horses barely touch the floor as she sprints over. I'm pretty stiff when people hug me, and I take a step back. The last time I saw Naomi was at her father's memorial service, where she had shrunk into a twisted ball of sadness. Today, her head is held high, and her chin's out, friendly and fierce. Her hundred-watt green eyes and 110-watt smile light her up and make me smile right back.

"Bosco!" Lilly shouts from the van area.

"Rosco!" Naomi shouts back.

They grab each other's hands and twirl around, chanting "Matolly, Matolly." That's the sleepaway camp where they made up those dumb nicknames.

Dad gives Naomi a big hug. "What a wonderful surprise! How's your mom?" he asks in a shaky voice. He's mostly not an emotional person, but tears streamed down his cheeks at the memorial for his best friend, Kyle.

"Ruth has good days and bad days," Naomi says. She likes to call her parents by their first names. She forces herself to smile. "She's making sculptures again and got a job at an art gallery in Litchfield." She looks over at the van workshop area. "And how about you guys? Ruth says you're working on the van again."

"It's going great," Dad says.

"Come on," Lilly says. "Take a look."

The van with its steel frame exposed reminds me of the dinosaur skeletons in the Museum of Natural History. The van's body, or "skin," with solar panels is attached to a crane high above and will be lowered onto and attached to the frame when the time comes. Until then, the gauges, wires, and electric motors by each wheel are exposed, making them easy to work on.

Do I see disappointment on Naomi's face? Dad must have read her reaction too. "I know it looks like we're not very far along," he says. "But we're pretty close to getting the whole thing put together."

Naomi jumps into the driver's seat and runs her fingers over the dashboard. "Do you need help? I learned a lot about mechanical stuff working on the XKE and my go-karts with Kyle."

"Of course," Dad says.

"Yeah!" my sister shouts. "We're installing brakes today."

Naomi pulls a wrench off the wall, where tools are neatly organized on brackets. "Then we'll need this brake bleeder."

Lilly and Naomi high-five.

I'm at my computer desk, not concentrating on code because I'm watching Lilly and Naomi laughing and singing along with the radio.

Why does Naomi seem so happy? Didn't her father's death make her sad and angry? It certainly made my dad feel that way.

Mom thinks whatever sunny optimism Dad had died when his best friend and business partner passed away. He became supercritical of Lilly and me. We were slackers because we didn't get perfect scores on every test and homework assignment. I slouched too much, and even when I did stand up straight, it wasn't good enough for him. Mom got the same treatment. He complained that the food she cooked tasted terrible, and the apartment was always filthy.

I used to put a pillow over my head so I wouldn't hear them arguing about how harshly he treated Lilly and me. They also fought about his fixation on Kyle's list of things he really wanted to see and do but never could because he died so quickly from cancer.

Dad decided to honor his friend by seeing the objects, visiting the places, and doing the activities on Kyle's list. Mom called his undertaking a fool's errand—a waste of time. The shouting about this got loud and frequent, and eventually, Dad left our family for three and a half months. At least I didn't have to put a pillow over my head to block out their angry voices anymore.

When he got back, he was eager to tell us all a story. Mom wasn't so interested, but Lilly and I were. The last item on his list was to climb Denali, the tallest mountain in Alaska. "It was the hardest thing I've ever done," he told my sister and me. "I hired a guide, and it took us twelve days to reach a camp near the summit, where we rested so our bodies could adjust to the thin atmosphere. We struggled to the top in the darkness. As the sun slowly rose, I experienced an overwhelming emotion that released me from the sadness and negativity that had haunted me since my friend's death. Now I can celebrate his life, not just mourn him. Kyle would be delighted that I'm eager to discover something good in each new day and every person."

I think Lilly and I are included in "every person." Since he got back, Dad has been more encouraging and less critical. But he and Mom still argue, so he's living here in his Amish house and doesn't come with Lilly and me when we take Naomi back to our apartment for dinner.

# CHAPTER 4

**MOM'S SO HAPPY TO SEE** our guest that she lets us order Naomi's favorite spicy Indian takeout. Great! Now I don't have to pretend I like the leftover meatloaf.

While we're eating, Mom asks Naomi what she'll do after we finish building the solar-powered van.

"I'm going to race car driving school, Aunt Jean."

Mom's not really her aunt, but our families are so close that we're like relatives.

"That's kick-ass, girl," Lilly says.

"Where's the school?" Mom asks.

"England. Drivers from all over the world come to the Sussex Open Wheel Racing School because it's the best."

"Very adventurous." Mom's quicker with praise than my dad.

"I just have to win one more kart race here in America to qualify for the program," Naomi says. "And then I have to come up with the money for tuition somehow."

I can't picture Naomi being a race car driver. Many sixteen-year-olds in the city don't even have driver's licenses because it's 87 percent challenging to drive in horn-honking city traffic. The kids at my school mostly plan to go to Ivy League universities to become computer engineers, doctors, or lawyers. Lilly wants to be an astronaut.

My sister and Naomi squeeze into our tiny kitchen to do the dishes. It's incredible how they gab away and laugh at each other's unfunny jokes like they've seen each other every day. But Naomi and her mom moved to the country after her father died over a year ago.

And, it doesn't really make sense that they're best friends because they're so different. My sister hardly ever gets angry. Well, sometimes, but not enough to punch someone in the face like I saw Naomi do when a foul-mouthed boy was bothering her. Often, I don't know what Lilly's thinking behind her smile; it could be friendly or not, like my dad. But joy and sadness are easy to see on Naomi's face. My sister is a brainiac—number one in her grade—and I've heard that Naomi has learning challenges.

Maybe she and Naomi are friends because they share interests that Mom calls "unfrilly." Lilly is on the robotics team at school and recklessly rollerblades down hills in Central Park. Naomi knows what to do with a brake bleeder wrench and races go-karts.

I leave Bosco and Rosco and challenge my best friend Luke to a chess game on the computer. He's ahead when the monitor goes dark and all the lights go out.

Mom comes in. "A blackout!"

The city's never totally dark because of streetlamps and the glow from apartment and store windows. Now the only light outside my window comes from car headlights. I check my phone, and there's no cell service.

"Let's go out and see what's going on," Lilly says.

Naomi's excited to go too.

The adventurer girls, Mom, and I head into the night.

Our building superintendent and his wife, who are sitting on our front stoop, have no information about the blackout. I'm sweating a little because even at 10:04, it's ninety-two degrees. Some families have brought folding chairs onto the sidewalk, where it has to be cooler than their un-air-conditioned apartments. Everyone has their phone flashlights on.

"All the lit screens look like fireflies," Mom says. She grew up in the suburbs, where real fireflies like it better than on West Eighty-Second Street.

We stop by a crowd gathered around a parked car, listening to its radio. I hear the reporter announce that much of upper Manhattan and half of Queens are without electricity and cell service. Amazing!

No one seems tense or frightened, not even I. A zooming posse of skateboarders celebrates the darkness by howling like coyotes. Naomi sprints alongside them for a few steps and howls too. A man wearing a giant cowboy hat is directing traffic at a Broadway intersection because the traffic lights are out. He stops the cars so the wild skaters can continue their stampede.

"Lilly!" It's her other best friend, Whitney. How can you have two best friends? Doesn't *best* mean unequaled? Whitney and some kids from our school are all talking and laughing at the same time. My sister and Naomi wave for me to join them.

I hesitate. "You know her friends from when they come to the apartment, Seb," Mom says. "You look like you want to join them. Go on."

She's right because she's right a lot. She can't spin her head 270 degrees like a real owl, but she's owl-wise. But my sister says I'm as spontaneous as a rocket launch, where everything is planned down to the second, years in advance, and I haven't thought about what I would talk about with those kids. So I say, "Mom, you might not be aware that those preppy kids are really the notorious West Side Gang, who steal and sell drugs and murder little children."

My mom blows out a frustrated breath.

In our apartment, Mom stretches on a yoga mat by the light of a candle.

She does one last bendy thing and stands, her hands resting on her lower back. "Better." She injured it when she was riding in a cab that crashed, and she had to do physical therapy for eleven months.

"Great," I say.

"You know I have to do stretches every day to keep my muscles strong and flexible." She drinks some water. Here comes the lesson.

"I don't have to decide whether I do it or not. It's automatic now—a habit." Another sip. "There are techniques to overcome shyness. If you do them every day, they'll become a habit. I can practice with you so you'll be able to open new doors to try new things and make new friends."

She can push and poke me, and sometimes this makes me use her big words against her. "You think I'm an invalid."

"Oh, honey. I certainly do not." "You don't think I could become like Lilly in a second if I wanted to?"

"Sebastian, I—"

"I can do it myself." I don't yell or anything, but I go to my room and shut the door. I sit by my open window, hoping for a cooling breeze. I want to share my expedition into the blacked-out streets with Luke, but I can't contact him because there's no cell or internet service. Like the little prince on the cover of his book, I'm standing on a planet somewhere in space. Alone.

# CHAPTER 5

**I'M AT MY DESK** in the Innovation Factory, so obviously the power is back.

On my phone, I'm reading that heat lightning struck a large generator to cause the blackout and how the electric company fixed it before dawn, when the doorbell rings. Dad quickly buzzes the front door open like he's been waiting for someone.

Yes, he has been because it's Mom. She waves a quick hello to me and goes directly into Dad's house. The simple Amish door closes to keep out my prying eyes and ears.

Pretty much the only thing that can get my parents together in the same room these days is something they are both concerned about: *me*. Wondering what they're plotting makes it hard to concentrate on my coding.

I go over to the van area, where Naomi has just finished hanging posters with photos of a dark-haired woman wearing a pink-and-green racing suit. She's posing next to a race car with her chin thrust forward under warrior! in big letters. In another poster, she's relentless.

"Who's that?" I ask.

"Danica Patrick. The best woman race driver in the world," Naomi tells me.

"And when Never-Lose Naomi starts to drive real race cars, she'll be on posters too," Lilly says.

Has Naomi really never lost a race?

"What kind of posters are you going to be on, Sebastian? What's your dream?" Naomi asks.

I shrug.

"He's going to build the world's fastest computer and use it to create a miracle cancer-curing drug," my sister boasts for me.

"With those big blue eyes and rosy cheeks, he's too cute to be really smart. How about being a TV star?" Naomi says, sharing a grin with my sister.

I'm 100 percent blushing because my cheeks always burn pink at a compliment. "My dream is that I won't be afraid to have a dream," I whisper.

They both lean closer. I say it a little louder.

"A good start to the race," Naomi says.

I go back to my computer, but I'm still watching the perfect house door out of the corner of my eye. Then, finally, Mom comes out like she's late for a meeting, except she's never late for anything. "I just had some money stuff to talk about with your father," she says in her it's-not-a-harmful-lie voice.

What have my parents schemed up?

Harold talking to himself interrupts my thoughts. "Yeahhh. Yeahhh." He often says things twice.

He texts me, telling me to come watch his new video. He likes to digitally put himself into actual movies and TV shows so he can be the hero. He shoots down enemy fighter planes or protects pretty women from villains. Dad calls these fantasies "Harold World."

In this one, he gets out of a shiny convertible near a small jet. He's a lot thinner than in real life and athletically jogs up the plane's folding stairs. The inside is like a living room with big sofa seats, and Harold sits in the biggest one. Pretty ladies bring him food on a silver plate and a glass of something with lots of bubbles. *Livin' large!* he texts.

"You look good," I tell him like I've told him before. He nods, agreeing with me, and he's still nodding when I go back to my desk.

When Lilly and I come into the warehouse the next day, Dad and Naomi are quietly talking as they pick up stuff from the floor in the van area.

I can't hear what they're saying, but I see him point at me. Then Dad pulls out his cell phone. "I have to take this," he says and strides into his house to talk in private. Lilly starts to work installing electrical wires in the van, and Naomi goes to the parts bins, where she writes something on a pad.

"Sebastian!" she yells. "Get over here and have some fun." She can be pretty loud.

Fun? I might as well see what she thinks is fun.

"Uncle Arthur dropped this part." She shows me the broken pieces. "He says you're a whiz on the 3D printer and can make a new one." She hands me a scrap of paper with a number written on it. "This is the part number."

My dad is one of the least clumsy people in the universe. I've never seen him drop anything. Is this what he and my mother schemed up? He deliberately breaks the part. Then he gets a call and hides out in his private office. Only I didn't hear his *da-da-da-dah* ringtone, the first four notes of a famous classical music thing Uncle Kyle liked. So maybe the call was spice—not real. Maybe he's plotting for me to spend time using the 3D printer near Lilly and Naomi. The two popular, outgoing young ladies will demonstrate how to become outgoing and popular to little old me, all in one afternoon.

Or maybe Dad's too busy to program the 3D printer himself. Plot or not, I nod.

The printer is the size of a small car with a computer attached. We can program it to make parts out of hard or soft plastic. I type in the number, and a picture of a bolt pops up on the monitor.

"That's not it," Naomi says.

I point to the number she gave me. "This is the number for the bolt you see on the monitor."

She goes to a parts bin and returns with a new number with the same digits in reverse order. She shrugs. "I sometimes get numbers and letters mixed up. I'm a little cix-el-syd." She laughs at what my loving sister calls my duh face. "That's dyslexic backward."

Ah. "A good e-koj," I say. She quickly understands that I have said "joke" backward and laughs. So do I. Naomi and my sister are more fun to be around than Harold.

I type in the correct number, and a part with holes in it appears on the monitor. "That's it. A wire harness." I'm sending its specifications to the printer when my phone rings.

"Want me to get it?" Naomi asks.

"Sure. It's probably a wrong number anyway. Nobody calls me except my mom." The printer hums and buzzes as nozzles precisely spray plastic in the shape of the part.

"Potential spam." Naomi cancels the call and stares at my lock screen. It's a picture of a bunch of teenagers. Pointing to a short guy at the edge of the group, she asks, "Is that you in old fashion clothes?"

"It's my dad before he had a growth spurt. He was the only freshman ever invited to be on the Amsterdam Academy math team. They won the New York State Math Challenge and then came in second nationally."

"You're going to be to move from the middle school to the high school at Amsterdam Academy this fall, aren't you?"

I nod.

"You're a turbo-boosted math genius. You'll be the second freshman to make the team."

"I have to … try out."

"What?"

Sometimes my voice fades away on words I'm nervous to even say. "I have to stand up in front of the team and answer difficult math questions."

"Then you'll have to ace it."

"My brain sometimes freezes when I have to talk in front of strangers, even when I know the answers."

Naomi moves so she's right below the posters of Relentless Danica. "People tell me girls aren't skilled or daring enough to win car races at the highest level, and I'm kind of a girl. I have to train harder to become faster and better than the boys. You can do the same."

"I'm a little shy."

"Yeah, yeah, you're shy. That's an excuse to not try, not a good reason. Kyle told me there are no excuses in life, Sebastian. It's what his father told him. Dare to make that math team. You'll be proud of yourself, and so will Uncle Arthur." She punches her open hand with a fist, an exclamation point. "Get unshy!"

# CHAPTER 6

**"TRUST ME,"** Luke says as we video chat on my work computer.

He's 100 percent the best at learning about anything by reading articles on the internet, so I trust his advice. Today, Luke wears a doctor's white coat that is so big it drags on the floor. "Does talking to me make you anxious?" he asks.

"No."

"Do you have difficulty talking to people you don't know?"

"A little." A lot.

"Do you attend social gatherings?"

"If you mean parties, I don't go to parties."

"Because you fear other kids or adults will judge you?"

"Maybe, but mostly I just don't have many friends, so I don't get invited to many parties."

"If you were an animal, what would you be?"

I could say a hawk because they're so beautiful and free. Or a seal like the playful ones in the Central Park Zoo. "I guess I'm kind of like a chipmunk."

"Because you're small, cute, intelligent, and solitary?"

Luke knows about animal behavior like I do. I nod.

"Hey, dude," a robot voice interrupts. It's the android that Dad and Uncle Kyle developed to answer tourists' questions in

Hawaii. They modeled her on a native woman wearing a grass skirt and holding a ukulele, and they named her Aloha Alice. Her eyes are cameras that "see," and her computer-generated voice can speak in fifteen different languages. Harold uses a joystick to guide her around the warehouse on motorized wheels.

He sometimes gets his words jumbled when talking directly to people, so he programmed Alice to speak what he types into his computer or cell phone. It can be pretty funny to hear his Darth Vader–deep voice coming out of the female robot's mouth.

My sister thinks a big hairy bear man using a lady bot to express himself makes Harold odder than the scientists in *The Big Bang Theory*. Maybe, but he's nice too.

"What up with the questions?" he asks, peering into his phone screen. He sees what Alice "sees": Luke in a white doctor's coat on my monitor. Harold types furiously, and then his raspy computer voice says, "Ah, a headshrinker, headshrinker." *Headshrinker* is what he calls a psychologist or a psychiatrist.

"I'm … we're figuring out ways to become unshy."

More typing. "Unshy. Yes, yes. Shyness is a heavy burden. Can't fly if you got shy weighing you down, down." The way Harold says "shy" sounds like the swear word for poop. "Headshrinkers shrink heads. What you need … what you need is a head-sweller."

Alice glides away.

Luke agrees with Harold. "But it wouldn't be fun if your head swelled so big it exploded."

# CHAPTER 7

**"NICELY DONE,"** Dad says.

He and I are in the van area, where he inspects the part I created on the 3D printer. His compliment doesn't swell my head enough to blow up, though it does make me smile.

"You want to help us build the van, Sebastian? We could use your computer skills."

I'd have to make a whole list of stuff to talk about with Lilly and Naomi. "I'll think about it."

"Don't overthink. Overthinking becomes fretting."

I'm eating a peach and video chatting with Luke.

"What do you think?" I ask.

"First, no more fretting. Recent medical research shows that fretting can put you into a mental rut from which it is challenging to extricate yourself." Sometimes Luke talks like he's reading research out loud. "I think there would be a positive outcome if you did work with the more extroverted girls."

I guess I agree. "Okay."

"And don't forget, when you greet them, bow low and say, 'Bonjour, *mademoiselles*. How can I be of service?'"

I bow very low in front of Naomi and Lilly, then force myself to look them in the eyes.

"*Bonjour, mademoiselles.* How can I be of service?"

They're laughing. At me? I look down.

"Sebastian, have you been reading some frilly romance novel from two hundred years ago?" Lilly asks as she curtsies.

I realize Luke must have researched not-very-modern books on shyness, and I laugh like I intended it to be a joke.

"The directional blinkers aren't working," Naomi says. "We can check the wiring connections. Can you be of service and see if there's a bug in the software?"

I nod.

Almost everything in the van is controlled by computer software with a gazillion lines of code. The best way to search for defects is to write a program to search for a bug. I hum my favorite song along with Luke, who's on my phone.

"I've never heard that before," Naomi yells over.

I tell her what it is but too softly.

"You gotta make it loud, dude, or the world won't care about you." Critical and encouraging at the same time. Did Lilly advise Naomi to nudge me out of my shyness?

"It's this song called 'I *Love My Dog*.'"

"But what's the fun part, Seb?" Lilly asks.

My sister' is nice because she knows what the fun part is but lets me tell it. "The guy singing is named Cat. Cat Stevens."

"That's funny. Is he the cat meowing along with you?" Naomi asks.

"No. That's my friend Luke."

"His voice is strange."

Is she suspicious? "He has a cold," I tell her.

# CHAPTER 8

**LUKE HAS SUGGESTED SOME TECHNIQUES** for how to meet new people.

I'm in our apartment bathroom, practicing looking into my own eyes and saying my name over and over in a clear, loud voice. I have the shower going so Mom doesn't get all upset that I'm talking to myself like a crazy person on the street.

"Are you talking to yourself in there?" sonar-ears Mom asks.

"I'm practicing for glee club."

"Glee club?"

She's right, I am a terrible singer. "I can get better if I practice, Mom."

"Well, Brendon and Mrs. Spitz are here. Please come out and say hello."

These are the new people. Brendon will be entering ninth grade at Amsterdam Academy in the fall, and he won't know anyone. Plotter Mom has arranged for me to meet him so I can show him around when school starts.

Brendon's kneeling on the living room floor, petting my dog, and barely looks up when I say hi. He reminds me of a colt. Not that he's wobbling on unsteady legs, but he seems so uncertain.

His mother has worry lines on her forehead as she watches him. "Brendon likes your dog," Mrs. Spitz says, talking for her son.

I smile at her because I know how Naomi's smile made me smile, and Mrs. Spitz smiles back. "Hi, I'm Sebastian Kemp," I say, loud and clear.

Luke has also advised me to shake hands firmly because that shows character. I squeeze hers so hard she flinches.

Then Brendon and I sit on the sofa, listening to the ladies chitchat, and I'm already 79 percent bored.

"Why don't you show Brendon your room?" my mom suggests. Sometimes it's like she thinks I'm furniture she can just move around.

It doesn't take long to show him my closet-sized bedroom. Above a corkboard full of photos and chess ribbons are posters of the great Yankees right fielder Aaron Judge and Jedi knight Luke Skywalker.

Brendon whispers, "Go Yankees!" to Aaron Judge and "Come to the dark side" to Luke. I guess it's nice that we both like baseball and Star Wars. He points to a picture of our family eating in a room where the walls and ceiling are curved. "Where's that?"

"An old plane they made into a restaurant at the airport. Pretty dumb, but good French fries."

Lucky comes in and hops up on my bed, where Brendon pets him some more. Maybe he's more comfortable with animals than with humans like I am sometimes. "My father won't allow us to have a dog," Brendon tells me. "They mess up everything when they shed."

Brendon looks at my computer, then looks away like he's embarrassed for me. "I know it looks like a pile of junk, but it's superfast," I tell him. "My dad and I made it from special parts we ordered."

Next to it is a sudoku puzzle book. Mom the teacher and

Mom the mom don't believe in wasting brain cells, so there's no shortage of educational material around here.

Brendon opens it to a new puzzle and nods like he wants to solve it. We each attack one, and Brendon finishes as fast as I do. We're just starting new ones when the moms come in, all apologetic for interrupting our fun. It's time for them to go.

"See you in school," I say.

Brendon nods and half-smiles at the floor. I think he's shyer than me.

After they leave, Mom comes back into my room. "You're lucky to have someone in your class who can keep up with you mentally," she chirps. "I'll give you Brendon's phone number if you want to get together before school starts."

Is this chapter two of the plotting?

"And can I offer a suggestion?" This sounds like a question but really isn't. "You don't need to crush someone's hand when you shake it, and you can say your name in a normal voice, not a shout."

Will the plotting never end?

I grin at her and yell, "Okay!"

I get a grin back. "You're trying, aren't you?"

I nod. But just becoming unshy won't get me on the math team.

I'm sitting in my bedroom with my legs curled up underneath me, practicing for the math team and grilling on my phone with Luke.

"Go on, ask me a hard one," I say.

"Do you like your new friend?"

"He's okay, and that's not a hard question."

"Maybe harder than you understand right now. Do you think there will be a time when you like him more, and you will forget about me?"

"What are you talking about? You're my best friend."

"Anyway, what's the sum of the first ten prime numbers?"

Definitely not too easy. I close my eyes and visualize those numbers.

"Your friend still has a cold," Naomi says, startling me. She and my sister have snuck into my room. Or maybe they just walked in normally; when I'm concentrating, I don't hear anything except what's in my head.

"What do you think of Naomi's new protective racing suit?" Lilly asks. It's a bright green tight-fitting bodysuit with pink parts along the shoulders and down her side. Naomi poses like her idol with a confident, grown-up smile that's friendly and fierce at the same time.

"Great!"

"We're going to test-drive the van for the first time tomorrow and want to make sure our driver looks sharp," Lilly says.

"Getting ready for the audition?" Naomi asks.

I nod.

"Where will it be?"

"Somewhere in the school, I guess."

"Probably in classroom one seventeen," Lilly tells us. "A lot of auditions take place there because it has a raised area like a stage."

"You'll have to stand, won't you?" Naomi asks me.

"I guess."

"Lilly, does he look all coiled up like he's trying to be invisible?"

"Or hide."

"Sebastian, try standing up to answer your friend's questions," Naomi suggests.

I uncurl my legs and get up. Naomi steps closer to me, and my throat tightens, and my face must stiffen too. "Easy, big guy, I'm not going to smack you." She straightens my shoulders and uses a finger to tilt my chin up a little. "Stick your chest out. Challenge those dudes."

Standing taller like this actually releases some tightness in my shoulders, and I feel more relaxed. "Ask me another hard question, Luke."

He doesn't, and I see that he has ended the call. That's probably a safe idea. "His phone probably ran out of battery," I say.

"Okay. How much is seventeen plus eighty-three?" Naomi asks.

"The questions are going to be a lot harder than that."

"What kinds of questions do you expect?" my sister asks.

"Like, determine the sum of the first ten prime numbers."

"What is a prime number?" Naomi wants to know.

"A number that's divisible only by one and itself. Like three or seventeen."

"Okay, smarty-pants, add the first ten of those things."

Mom calls from the kitchen, "Food is on the table."

"One hundred and twenty-nine," I answer correctly to myself.

But nobody hears me because the ladies have headed for the dining room table.

# CHAPTER 9

**WEARING HER GREEN-AND-PINK RACING SUIT**, Naomi jumps behind the steering wheel of the van.

Lilly climbs into the seat next to her. I stand on the metal chassis and hold on to the back of the driver's seat. Nearby, Dad watches, along with Aloha Alice. Harold has activated its video camera eyes so he can witness the event from his desk. Naomi punches the start button, and the van's dashboard lights up. "Hear that?"

"I don't hear anything," I answer.

"Right. Electric motors are almost silent," she says and pushes the accelerator down. The van jumps forward so quickly I almost fall backward.

"Wow," she laughs. "So baaad! Did you know an all-electric car raced a turbocharged German sports car and left it in the dust? Electric rules!"

She presses the accelerator more gently this time, and we glide around the entire warehouse floor, past the computer desks and the 3D printer. Huge grins light up all our faces.

"Are we ready to lower the body onto the chassis, Dad?" Lilly asks.

"Absolutely."

"I gotta spin out on you now," Naomi says.

"You're ditching us?" Lilly asks.

"I promised Victoria I'd walk Socks." Socks is the dog owned by the woman whose apartment Naomi is staying in. "Seb, why don't you get Lucky and meet us in the park?"

Did my dad suggest this to them? Maybe they're just being friendly. I agree because I won't have to chat with Naomi. I can talk with the dogs.

I meet Lilly and Naomi at the pond near the 103rd Street entrance to Central Park.

Socks has dark gray fur with three white paws. Socks, of course. He and Lucky sniff each other and wag their tails. It's not so easy to make friends with humans.

Socks is a mixed breed, and he pulls so hard on his leash that Naomi struggles to hold him even though I can see she's strong. "Is it okay if I walk him?" I ask.

"He's almost as big as you," Naomi says.

"But I'm smarter."

I have Lucky's leash in one hand and Socks' in the other. I've trained Lucky to walk gently by my side. Socks tugs, and I jerk the leash softly backward. I don't have to do this many times before he understands, or mostly understands, and trots beside us.

"How did you get him not to pull?" Naomi asks.

"He's a pack animal and wants to be part of Lucky's pack. But he forgets when he smells something too delicious to miss, like another dog's poop, or he sees a squirrel he wants to munch on. I just remind him with a firm tug."

"You've got the mojo," Naomi says.

"With dogs, maybe." Not with people.

I imagine I'm on the Math Olympics stage.

*The three judges glare at me.* "Down!" *I command.*

*They lie on the floor.* "Good boy. Good boy. Good girl," *I say.* "No *growling. No showing teeth. We're going to be friends.*" *They look at me with big round eyes that beg for affection. I say in a clear voice,* "Bring on the questions!"

"Sebastian," I hear. I feel someone gripping my arm. It's Naomi. "You let the dogs go into the pond, and now they're covered with slime. They almost pulled you in with them."

"What were you dreaming?" Lilly asks.

"Nothing." But the image of the obedient judges on the floor makes me smile.

"We'll have to wash them off on Victoria's patio," Naomi says. She's staying in the building where her family used to have an apartment.

Lilly and Naomi walk ahead, and I can't hear what they're whispering. Is that because they're saying negative things about me? Luke has advised me that, contrary to what I think, people don't always talk just about me. My friend isn't uncritical all the time.

In the elevator up to Victoria's apartment, Naomi tells us, "You'll really like Ms. Natural. Everything in her apartment and all her clothes are made from natural materials. Kyle thought up the nickname, and Victoria liked it so much she changed her email to MSnatural."

Ms. Natural thinks it's oh-so-amusing that the dogs almost pulled me into the pond. She helps us wash them with a hose on her apartment's terrace and doesn't mind when her peacock-colorful all-natural clothes get soaked.

We go to the kitchen for a snack, and it's a long walk because the apartment is so big. The fresh organic pear Victoria gives me is maybe the best thing ever.

"Do you still have the sexy green car?" she asks Naomi.

"The XKE? For sure."

"I visited Kyle, Ruth, and Naomi in the country and went to the grocery store with her father in that convertible," she tells Lilly and me. "Oh my lord, he drove a hundred and sixty miles per hour on those curvy country roads! I've never been so terrified in my life! Promise me you will drive me around at a hundred and sixty after you graduate from racing school, Naomi."

"I'll put the hammer down for you!" she promises.

Victoria gushes about how the solar-powered van will decrease both carbon and noise pollution. Cities around the world will be more people-friendly when more things are solar-powered.

Everything is either the best or the worst for Ms. Natural. The way her voice rises and falls to emphasize things and how she talks with her hands remind me of Lilly's friend who wants to be an actress on Broadway. "When will you be finished?" Victoria asks.

"I'm not really sure," Lilly says. We're having problems getting some of the parts we need."

"What specific parts?"

"The voltage isolator relays to connect the solar panels to the batteries and a replacement hard drive."

Victoria crooks a finger and presses it against her mouth so we understand she's deep-thinking. "Well, how can you save the world without those replays things? I absolutely have to witness the future."

# CHAPTER 10

**"IT'S GORGEOUS,"** Victoria declares.

Before she arrived, we lowered the outer body onto the van and polished the solar panels until they sparkled.

Dad explains how the panels will convert sunlight into electricity to power all the van's electronics and motors. Excess energy will be stored in high-efficiency batteries so the van can operate at night and on cloudy, rainy, and snowy days.

"Brilliant, Arthur. Compared to the air-polluting, ugly, box-on-wheels delivery trucks, this is a work of art! Kyle would be proud." She looks at Naomi. "Proud of you all."

Victoria looks around the van lab. "Arthur, Naomi was educating me about your building process. I would be delighted to see what a voltage isolator thing actually looks like."

"They're still on order," he tells her.

"Is there a problem with shipping?" she asks.

"There's a discrepancy in our bank account. I'm straightening it out."

Victoria does the thinking thing again with her bent finger. "Do you have a minute? There's something I'd like to discuss."

"Of course," Dad answers. "Why don't we go into my office."

He uses the dining room with its unpainted wooden table and four straight-back chairs as his private meeting space. Ms. Natural will probably think this is also "gorgeous."

"Naomi, would you join us?" Victoria asks.

Lilly and I study the Amish house. "What do you think they're talking about?" I ask.

"When grown-ups close doors, it's usually to worry about their kids or their money," my big sister says. "I'd say it's money this time."

In just over fifteen minutes, Naomi bounds out of the house with a 110 percent grin brightening her face as she grabs Lilly's hands and spins them both around. Harold steers Aloha Alice over to join us, so he must be curious what's making her so happy too.

Naomi's words tumble out of her in such an excited rush that she's not really making sense. Something about Victoria buying part of Naomi's family's shares in the business and providing money to complete building the van and to develop a marketing plan. Uncle Arthur called Ruth in the country, and she happily agreed to this deal.

I don't totally understand what she's talking about. Harold types energy-drink fast at his computer. Then Alice says, "They made a deal so there will be moolah-moolah to buy the parts you need and to pay for Naomi's racing school tuition in England."

"You go, Bosco!" Lilly shouts.

"You go, Rosco!" Naomi shouts back.

But doesn't Bosco have to win one more race to get accepted? What if she doesn't?

# CHAPTER II

**RACE CARS ROCKET ACROSS THE SCREEN** of a computer propped up on the solar van's dashboard.

The video shows what must be the driver's view out the windshield. Naomi grips the van's steering wheel as if she is actually driving the race car. "This is what, the hundredth time you've watched that?" Lilly kids.

"Get real. It's only the ninety-second."

The cars are going 129 percent fast. "Is this a race you drove in?" I ask.

"Danica films every race," Naomi says. "This is the IndyCar Japan 300, her first big win. I'm studying when she hits the brakes going into a corner and then accelerates out of it." She demonstrates by stomping on the van's brakes then jerking its steering wheel as the race car goes into a turn. "This is how I'll become the next relentless warrior."

Another car blocks Danica on a straight part of the track. Naomi's on the edge of her seat, knees pumping. "Now! Attack!" Naomi says just as Danica swoops in front of the car to cross the finish line first. Naomi raises her fist in victory as if she were driving.

"Going so fast looks like a total hoot," Lilly says.

"I don't have million-dollar race cars in our Connecticut barn, but I do have go-karts. I'm going home this weekend. Come with me. They're super fun to bomb around in."

Lilly makes a frustrated face. "Oh ... I promised Whitney I'd go to Martha's Vineyard with her family."

"So you're ditching me for another friend?"

"Gotta go with the best offer."

They must be kidding because they both laugh.

"How about you, Seb? It's a lot more exciting than sitting in front of your computer."

I'm a city kid. I've never really thought about driving anything except maybe a million-dollar subway train.

"Come on. Speed will be your friend," she promises.

# CHAPTER 12

NAOMI'S HOUSE IN THE COUNTRY is surrounded by open fields and woods with no other homes in sight.

How safe can it be here?

Dad drives Naomi and me up the long dirt driveway to a farmhouse with a barn. It might be old, but it looks pretty nice, with red shutters, peachy-colored walls, and flower gardens that could give me hay fever.

Naomi hops out of the car, and a border collie mix jumps up on her, wiggling excitedly. Then he greets me by putting his paws on my chest.

"Down, Luna," Naomi says, not really meaning it.

I pet him, and with each stroke, the tension eases out of my body. Dogs are better than medicine.

Naomi's mother, Ruth, comes out of the house and gives her daughter a hug. She shakes hands with me because she remembers I don't like hugs, and I remember not to squeeze her hand too hard. Ruth hugs Dad for a long time. "Good to see you, Arthur."

"Good to see you too, Ruth."

"Kyle would love that Naomi's working with you to finish the van." She rubs her cheek on his shoulder, maybe to wipe away a tear.

"She's a great kid," he says.

"Come on," Naomi says to me. "I want to show you something." She sprints away, and I chase her with Luna bouncing along beside us.

Behind the barn is a dirt road. "It's a shorter version of the racetrack at Le Mans, France, with the same turns and straightaways. Kyle and I built it."

Colorful metal signs for old-fashioned gas stations, boxy cars, and cabins called "motor courts" decorate the exterior walls. "Mom's art collection," Naomi says as she tugs open the big sliding door.

Inside, three pink-and-green go-karts with the number seven painted on the front are parked in a row. Next to them is a convertible with its top down, the real version of the model car Dad has in his kitchen.

The barn walls are painted bright white. Wrenches, screwdrivers, and other tools sit in brackets above metal worktables. Dad sometimes calls the van work area at the Innovation Factory "Kyle's operating room" because of the precise, clean way his partner organized it. This workspace is just like that.

"Welcome to my Maranello." She points to a poster of the shiniest, reddest race car decorated with a prancing black horse logo on its side. The car is parked in front of a factory with a giant sign that says ferrari. "They build the best race cars in the world in Maranello, Italy." There are more posters of Danica, naturally.

Naomi tosses me a helmet. "Let's have some fun!"

I hesitate. "I can't drive one of those go-karts."

"Of course, you can. You put your right foot on the accelerator and your left foot on the brake. It's simple."

"But I might crash."

"That's an excuse, not a reason. Come on."

I'm like those metal filings the science teacher uses to demonstrate magnetism. When a magnet comes close, the metal bits can't escape its pull, just like I can't escape Naomi's power. So I pull on the helmet.

She turns on the engines in two karts and zooms out of the open barn door before I even have my seat belt buckled. I jerk forward, stop, and jerk forward again onto the dirt track, where I push down on the accelerator. The kart picks up speed. My seat is only inches above the ground, and I'm sure I'll crash any second, so I slow almost to a stop at each turn. Naomi doesn't.

She rockets around a corner ahead of me so fast her kart spins around 180 degrees. A big grin brightens her face. "It'll catch you if you don't go faster."

I look back. There's nothing behind me. "What will?"

She roars off without answering.

On a straight part of the track, I "put the hammer down." The ground whizzes by. My heart is racing. My palms are sweating. This is sort of how I react when I stand too close to the edge of a tall building. Only in the kart, I'm also excited. I press the accelerator down more. Faster!

The straight part ends in a sharp turn, and I push the brakes down hard but not hard enough. The kart skids sideways to a stop. Dirt swirls around me. My hands are shaking, but I laugh. A nervous laugh but still a laugh. Whew!

Naomi skillfully spins her kart next to mine and pulls off her helmet. I do too.

"How much fun was that!" she yells.

"Ninety-one percent."

In the barn, Naomi takes the outer body off her kart.

She may get numbers backward and have trouble reading, but she's a genius with her hands. Not a wasted motion. She never picks up the wrong tool.

"Getting ready for the race?" I ask.

"I'm putting a larger chain sprocket on the engine, which should make the kart accelerate faster."

"They go fast enough for me."

"Top speed is only twenty."

"Feet per second?"

She laughs. "Miles per hour."

"It seemed a lot faster."

"Maybe because the karts are so low, so the track appears to just speed by."

"You need help?" I ask.

"I'll call if I need another set of hands."

Does she think I'm so clumsy I'll just get in the way?

I amble outside. It's a bright summer day. Not too hot. Not too chilly. I hear buzzing and hope it's not one of those South American wasps that can kill you with one sting.

Luna runs over, and I find a stick to play tug-of-war. He grabs one end, and I tumble to the ground, pretend-fighting. He growls, and I growl back as part of the game. Lucky and

I roughhouse like this. I don't fret about anything when I'm roughhousing with a dog.

Naomi joins us, and we both tug on the stick until Luna lets go, and we fall back onto the grass. She's laughing, then stops pretty suddenly as she looks up into the sky.

"See those straight white lines way up there? They're not clouds. They're contrails, exhaust from jets flying to Europe from New York."

"They must be very high because I don't see the planes."

"I'm scared, Sebastian." She takes my hand and this makes my hand shake a little, but I don't pull away because her's is trembling, too.

"I'll bet you've never been afraid of anyone or anything."

"I never sweat during a race. But just the idea of getting on an airplane ..." She points to her forehead, where beads of sweat are forming. "Kyle and I were once flying to a kart race in a small plane with only about twenty seats. It got caught in a thunderstorm, and the engines stopped, and we went straight down forever and ever. I grabbed Kyle's hand like it was the only thing keeping me alive. I'm here, so you know the pilots got the engines started and pulled out of the dive. But ... my father's not here to hold my hand now."

I try to think of something positive to say. "Isn't driving a race car ten times—maybe a hundred times—more dangerous than flying?"

"I know that in my head but not in my gut." She stands, petting Luna. "Anyway, I have a race to win."

She doesn't add, *But what if I don't win?* I'll have to remember to cut back on the buts and what-ifs.

# CHAPTER 13

**MY DAD AND I STAY OVER** in the country so we can watch Naomi race tomorrow.

After dinner, we're in the living room, where he's looking at a photo of a leaping tennis player hitting the ball. "It's impossible not to recognize sublime balance and grace." He sweeps his arm around. "You can feel Kyle here. The furniture, the art, the objects are all perfect in their own ways."

Scientist Dad sometimes talks the way emotional Uncle Kyle used to when describing his friend or Kyle's things.

He bends close to a coin inside a block of clear plastic. On one side is a picture of a warrior with what looks like a Roman helmet, so it must be ancient. On the other side is a design with eight spokes radiating out from a dot in the center. "It's a Roman solis, the sun coin. Isn't it beautiful?" Dad says as he studies it.

The deep rumble of a car engine seems to call to him, and he heads outside. I follow him to the front porch, and Ruth joins us just as the green convertible explodes out the open barn door with Naomi driving. Just before she's about to crash into the house, she expertly skids sideways to a stop.

"The 1968 Jaguar XKE," he says. "The most beautiful car ever made."

It's low to the ground and has curves in the front and back, so there are no bad angles. I don't know much about cars, but he might be right.

Naomi hops out and offers the key to Dad. "Kyle would want you to have it."

Dad looks exactly like I would in this situation: stunned and unable to find the right words or decide what to do.

"You know my damn optimist husband didn't have a will because he never imagined dying," Ruth says. She takes the keys from Naomi, puts them in Dad's hand, and squeezes his fingers closed around them. "Please don't reject our wish for you."

Dad stares at the car, smiling even though his eyes are watering. "I'll treat it with the utmost respect."

"We are certain of that," Naomi says. "And it doesn't have a rearview mirror."

I wonder what this means because the car does have a mirror so the driver can see what's behind.

Dad runs his hand over the body of the car like I would pet a friendly dog. He climbs in and speeds out of sight down the long dirt driveway. A loud screech alarms me. "Did he crash?" I wonder.

Naomi isn't worried. "That's just the sound of tires spinning on the paved road." She grins. "He put the hammer down!" Then she slaps her open palms together, apparently in appreciation.

The sun is down behind the low hills when Dad returns and parks the XKE inside the barn.

He's still sitting behind the wheel when Naomi and I come looking for him. She gets into the passenger seat and takes an envelope out of the glove compartment. "For the Art Dodger" is written on the outside.

"Until I met your father, I dodged any art," Dad explains. A ticket stub falls out of the envelope. "The Mauritshuis," he says to himself.

"What's that?" I ask.

"A museum in the Netherlands."

His eyes have the faraway look my mom says I get when I'm lost in a daydream or idea. Then he says, "Kyle was my roommate at MIT, and he was always searching for perfection. He found it in theorems, art, and processes like photosynthesis that confirmed his optimism. He believed these things were so flawless no one could deny their perfection. Of course, I disagreed. I believed in numbers and coding and finding flaws in things and ideas." *And children, sometimes,* I think. "Your father answered my pessimism with that wicked little smile he got when he knew something you didn't. He promised he'd prove me wrong but wouldn't tell me how or when."

Naomi shows us her version of that wicked little smile, and Dad's approving nod means she gets it right.

"The summer of our freshman year, we both had computer science internships at Oxford in England. But Kyle discovered this car that had been rotting in a country barn for twenty years, and he spent most of his time rebuilding the engine and restoring the body. When our internships were over, we headed to Italy to swim in the Adriatic and drink Chianti."

"And chase girls," Naomi adds.

Dad does his own version of the wicked little smile as he puts his hands on the steering wheel. "Traveling with him, you never knew where you'd wind up or what wonderful sight or interesting person you might chance upon. Right, Naomi?"

"My mom calls it Kyle-ing. He'd spot a church bell tower or something in the distance, and even if it were miles away from our destination, he'd chase it because it just might have a famous old painting or a beautiful gold altar inside."

"We were Kyle-ing through the Netherlands when he dragged me into the Mauritshuis to see a painting."

"*The Girl with the Pearl Ring*. No, the *Pearl Earring*," Naomi corrects herself. "Kyle took me there."

"He would have," Dad says. "That girl ..." He takes a deep breath. "She wasn't irresistibly beautiful, but the direct way she looked out pulled me into the painting." Dad leans forward like his body is remembering that feeling. "I moved from one side to the other, looking for a single flaw. But one more brushstroke or one less would have diminished the painting. I had not believed in perfection. And I had to admit I was wrong."

He turned to Naomi. "So I had to take the courses in art and literature and computer graphics Kyle picked for me. I realized I had avoided them because I was afraid of trying something new and difficult, making me a limited person. Your father opened my eyes and my mind."

He might have been looking at Naomi, but I'm pretty sure he was talking to me. Does he think that even if I try to make the math team I'll fail?

The shriek doesn't wake me.

I'm in a guest room, but it's too dark in the country to safely sleep. No friendly light from city streetlamps to keep my imagination calm. Luna helps a little. He's sleeping next to me on the bed.

A *half-human, half-beast wolf man prowls just outside the farmhouse until he finds the front door with the broken lock. He comes up the wooden stairs, making them creak like in a horror movie.*

I have to turn on the reading lamp to chase away that demon. Then the howl comes again. Luna's head pops up. Is it coming from *inside* the house? I hold on to the dog's collar and go into the hallway. The only light comes from Naomi's room. The door isn't closed all the way, and I peek in. Her body shakes as she watches a video on her laptop. Is she sobbing or laughing?

Luna noses the door open and nestles comfortingly against her. Dogs are the best. She senses I'm there and turns. Another wail makes me shiver. "Spooky, huh?" she says.

"It sounds like a wounded person in big-time pain. Police sirens are a lot more cheerful."

"It's a fisher cat hunting chipmunks and squirrels."

I've seen pictures of fisher cats in my animal books. They're like mink, only larger and very wild and fierce.

"I'm happy the fisher cat or the neighborhood serial killer isn't downstairs in the living room. Sorry to bother you." I back out.

"Want to see some happy videos of your dad when he was younger?"

It has to be better than listening to a beast torture squirrels. "Sure."

Dad and Kyle must have shot the video on their trip to Italy. They're both slim and hairy and do goofy stuff like jumping into the ocean in their clothes and drinking red wine for breakfast.

Another video pops up of Naomi and her father. She looks about ten, sitting on her father's lap as they plow the field with a tractor to make the racetrack. Father and daughter look like an experienced team of mechanics working on a kart in the barn.

"I really liked Uncle Kyle. I miss him a lot." This is true. He was always looking for the best in people. He would sometimes make friends with grown-ups who seemed like jerks because he would concentrate on their one or two good traits. Sometimes I try to do that too but mostly in my head. Before he died, Mr. B always encouraged me to not be afraid of taking on big challenges or analyzing complex problems. I guess I'm better at the problem thing right now than the other challenges. I miss both Mr. B and Uncle Kyle and get sad when I think of them. But Naomi's ache must be 100 percent more painful than mine.

"These videos actually make me happy," she says. She's smiling, but her eyes are moist. I offer her my just-in-case handkerchief, and she dries her tears then takes a deep breath. "But sad memories do chase me round and round like in a traffic circle sometimes." She makes a circular motion with her hand. "If I look in the rearview mirror, the sadness will keep me prisoner. So I put the hammer down to accelerate out of that sad circle. When I go fast enough, it can't catch me."

So this is what she meant this afternoon when she told me "it" was chasing me: sadness.

She whispers like she's telling me a secret, "Speed keeps me free."

# CHAPTER 14

*VARRROOOOOM.*

Ten go-karts speed by us, and Naomi is in fourth place. Ruth, Dad, and I cheer her on. We're at the straight part of the track, which then turns down a hill where the racers go out of sight. Go-fast Naomi passes other karts on just about every lap. Sadness doesn't have a chance to catch her today. Now she's right behind the leader, who has the shiniest kart.

"That's Prince Charles," Ruth says. "His family's rich, and he thinks that makes him—as my daughter says—a prince."

"How many more laps to go?" I ask.

Naomi's mom shakes her head. "Only one."

I clench my fists and urge her on by yelling, "GO!!!"

She can't hear me because the karts zip into a turn at the end of the straightway and disappear onto the back of the track, where we can't see them. Then the pack emerges onto the straightaway, with Charles in the lead and Naomi just behind him.

Terrible!

The prince crosses the finish line and raises his arm in victory as he steers into a parking area. Naomi doesn't slow down as she crosses the finish line, rockets into the parking area, and bangs her kart into Charles's. She yanks off her helmet and swings it viciously at him. "You forced me off the track!" She's a foot shorter than he is, but her ferocity makes the prince retreat.

Charles's father moves between the two teenagers. "Back off. You lost!"

As Dad and Ruth pull Naomi away, other teenage drivers and their parents gather around to see what the commotion is about.

Naomi shouts, "You banged into my kart! I was going into the lead, and you deliberately pushed me off the curve!"

"I had the perfect race line," Charles says with a smirk. "You tried to pass me on the outside, and you don't have the skill to keep from spinning out."

"Liar!"

A man with an official racetrack shirt comes over to Naomi. He bluntly tells her that race officials observed no illegal contact or blocking. End of story.

We all lift the kart onto the trailer behind Ruth's pickup truck and secure it for the ride back to the farm. Naomi paces around, muttering to herself. I hear a lot of swear words.

"She really wants to win," Dad says.

"More than wants. She *has* to win," Ruth says.

"Like her father."

"Like her father."

Naomi and I sit in the back seat as Dad drives us to New York.

Naomi is perfectly still but not calm. More like a clenched fist. Strange, because some part of her is almost always moving.

A foot tapping, a knee bouncing up and down, hands fiddling with a tool.

"There's only one more race this summer. What if I don't win it?" she wonders.

I tell Luke that Never-Lose Naomi lost. "Now she has a case of the what-ifs." Something I know a thing or two about.

"Maybe there is a way we can help her regain her confidence." Luke's always so positive.

Later that night, he emails me a digital video he has created. "I think she can drive faster than she has been," he tells me.

He searched the internet to learn everything about winning go-kart races, particularly on the track where she races in Connecticut. Then he created this video demonstrating the best "race line" into each corner, precisely when to apply the brakes before a curve and when to accelerate out of it. He put his video beside the one from her helmet cam from the race to show her where she could improve.

I don't know much about racing, but it looks like this could help her drive faster.

# CHAPTER 15

**THE TOPS OF NAOMI'S EARS** are angry red.

We're watching Luke's video at the Innovation Factory. It's plain that she jerks her kart into corners and out of them again. Luke's video demonstrates how her intensity slows her down, and a smoother technique would actually make her go faster. Luke has inserted messages: "Too much fierce brake, and easy on that angry punch to the accelerator," and "Breathe slowly."

She curses loudly at each correction. Dad, followed by the robot Aloha Alice, comes over to see what's bothering her.

We all watch Luke demonstrate that when she tried to pass Prince Charles on the wider outer part of the corner, she was going too fast, causing her kart to spin around. "The best way to pass is on the inside, closer to the corner's sharpest part," Luke advises. "Calmly fierce."

Naomi bangs her fist into the keyboard to stop the video. "Danica's a warrior. I drive relentlessly like she does. It's the way I win!"

*But you didn't win*, I say in my head. But maybe I whisper this out loud by mistake, because ...

"That asshole forced me off the track!" she yells at me. "The officials should have flagged Prince out of the race. I don't need a machine telling me how to drive!"

I hear Harold typing, and then Alice says, "He made it especially for you, for you."

"Who did?" she demands.

"Sebastian's friend Luke."

"LUKE ISN'T A HE! IT'S AN IT! LUKE'S A FRIGGING COMPUTER!" Naomi screams.

How does she know?

All eyes turn toward me. No one knows what to say, particularly me. There's no place to hide in the open warehouse space. I retreat into the bathroom and lock the door.

I know they're talking about me. Do I hear "It's so sad" and "Get the boy to a headshrinker," and "Pathetic, his only friend in the world is a robot"? Or is all that just in my head?

A gentle knock.

My dad asks me to come out. Maybe he knew Luke was digital all along. Maybe that's why he and Mom have been developing plots to help me make a friend. He calls to me again. What can I say? *Hi, Dad, aren't you proud of me because I don't need humans?*

Deep down inside, I knew this moment would come, but I thought I could make a joke of it. "Oh, I wanted a friend who was as loyal as a dog and didn't need to be house-trained." No one was going to LOL. Ever.

Another knock. "Sebastian, it's the total asshole, Naomi.

Will you talk to me?"

I won't.

"Please?"

Why should I make her feel better? I remain silent.

"I'm really sorry. I got angry at myself and took it out on you. I hate myself because I was cruel to my friend."

*You're not the only person who hates you*, I say in my head.

"You can't stay in there all day and all night, Sebastian."

I think: *I can stay until you're gone.*

After a long while, I don't hear any footsteps or whispers on the other side of the door. My phone is still on a table in the van lab, so I have no way of knowing how long I've been in here. It's late. My stomach's rumbling. It's later. Sleep has to be better than what's happening while I'm awake, so I slump down on the hard tile floor and close my eyes.

I must doze off because Aloha Alice singing *I Love My Dog*, accompanied by her ukulele, startles me awake. I crack open the door. Have Dad and Naomi given up on me as a hopeless case?

Only Harold is in the warehouse, and he's hunched over his computer keyboard, typing what he wants to say. "How would you describe Harold?" the robot says in Harold's deep voice. Harold doesn't ask, *How would you describe* me? He talks about himself like he's another person. As Lilly said, he's odd.

"Brilliant and creative," I say, talking to him, not Aloha Alice. "The animation you do for the video game is awesome. And you make me laugh with those videos where you put yourself into movies and TV shows."

"How old is he?"

What's Harold getting at? I'm not very good at judging the ages of grown-ups, but he's pretty old. "Thirty?"

"Thirty-three. Thirty-three. Do you think he'll ever be a star like in the videos he makes?"

I shrug. "Maybe."

More typing. "Harold has a genius IQ of one eighty-three," Aloha Alice tells me. "But he still lives in the little bedroom he had as a kid, and his mom still makes him Eggos for breakfast. His only friends are on the internet. He doesn't work to become less timid to be the guy with fast fast cars and supermodel girl-friends. Harold lives mostly in his head."

He types some more, and Alice plays a few chords on her ukulele in the meantime. Then Harold says, "I want to alert you. Humans are your inspiration and your friends, your friends, Sebastian. I'm Aloha Alice's prisoner. Beware of becoming me."

Even a bully wouldn't say something so painful about someone. "You're a nice person," I offer.

"You too, big guy."

I go to my desk to get my backpack. Naomi has left me a handwritten note, but I toss it into the trash rather than read it. I look over at Harold, hunched over his keyboard.

I thought he liked himself. He's definitely kind. He could have told me the same things other adults do: make friends, see a headshrinker, stop fretting about yourself, blah, blah. Instead, he warned me to *beware of becoming me*. It's like he cut himself open so I could see the weaknesses that keep him odd and lonely. No one has ever made it so clear what can happen if I live mostly in my imagination and avoid making human friends.

Riding the subway home, I'm so engrossed in wondering what Harold meant by "being a prisoner of Aloha Alice" that I go three stops past my station. I hop off the train and walk twenty-two blocks home. *Beware of becoming me* echoes in my brain. Harold said he lives mostly inside his head. I've never thought imagining things was negative. Was he saying if I continue, I'll wind up living with my mother when I'm thirty-three, eating waffles she cooks for me?

Maybe what makes Harold a little strange is not really his fantasies but that he uses Aloha Alice to talk for him. I've never needed Luke to speak for me. Yet.

I wish I could ask Mom or Dad advice about what to do about Luke, but sometimes parents just don't understand the super-important things. How about Lilly? She'll probably think I'm just as odd as Harold when she finds out about my robot. And I can't ask Luke what to do about Luke. I'll have to decide for myself.

I solve three separate mathematical formulas about what I should do with my digital friend. The answer to each one is the same. And the solution terrifies me.

# CHAPTER 16

**MY PARENTS MUST HAVE DONE** the share-the-bad-news-about-their-weird-son thing again because Mom makes my favorite pasta and picks up raspberry sherbet from the corner deli.

At dinner, she doesn't ask me to tell an amusing story about working on the solar van. My sister's still vacationing with Whitney, so there's no upbeat chitchat from her. In the 103 percent silence, our spoons clinking against our bowls are trash-truck loud.

Eventually, Mom breaks the silence. "A friend of mine has a theory that you never make a mistake in life." One hundred percent certain her "friend" is Dr. Pry and Poke, the psychologist.

"You learn from positive things and also from defeats and humiliations, Seb."

I have had both of those in one day and don't feel one byte smarter.

"You can figure out what went wrong and find ways to fix it so it won't happen again."

If I agree with her, maybe she'll stop. "Uh-huh," I mumble.

She forces her best gritted-teeth smile. "You should be proud of yourself for having the intelligence and skill to create a computer friend. How did you do it?"

"You don't really want to know."

"I'm sure there are only a handful of kids your age in the entire country who could create such a sophisticated AI person. So yes, I'm very curious how my twelve-year-old did it."

Phew. No point in keeping it a secret. "I started with the program Dad and Uncle Kyle created for Aloha Alice and coded it so Luke would sound like a teenage boy. Then I made him really smart by giving him access to the artificial intelligence program Harold and I use for the video game."

"Where did the name come from?"

"You know, Luke Skywalker from Star Wars."

"How dumb of me."

Never-dumb Mom always talks about the importance of good character and the three fundamentals she believes it's built on. I tell her, "I programmed Luke to research the essential qualities of curiosity and empathy and tenacity, then download them to use in his relationship with me. He never figured out how to comfort me when I'm sad like Lucky does, but we played high-level chess and math games. And he's good at researching stuff about shyness, which he used to coach me." I leave out that he never judges me or oozes disappointment.

"Really amazing."

I'm starting to feel not so bad. Maybe I am pretty smart.

"I have noticed a change in you, Seb. I think the stuff you worked on with Luke has been beneficial. What will you do with him now?"

I know what I have to do, and Luke has helped me gain the strength and confidence to do it. "I'll de ..." It's difficult to even say the word out loud. "I'll ... delete him. I'll delete *it*."

Mom reaches out to hold my hand. "My brave young man."

I'm sitting slump-shouldered at my bedroom computer, deleting the programs and data files I used to create Luke.

I'm usually a superfast, accurate typer, but I keep making mistakes tonight. Luke knows I'm destroying it, and yet it doesn't say "Goodbye, my friend," or "*Au revoir,*" or "Betrayed!" Nothing to make me sadder than I already am. But Luke does ask, "Can I pose a question?"

"Of course."

"You told me about Naomi and not looking in the rearview mirror, where she could see the sadness chasing her. What's chasing you?"

A challenging question. I have to think long and hard. I spin the planets on my mobile of the solar system. "I guess I'm scared I won't dare go to the math team audition."

"You've become more confident and less afraid since that day you left the Math Olympics at Stuyvesant High School.

Luke is such a great friend and advisor that I hesitate to delete any more of its memory. "Go on," it says. "You can do it."

Luke remains loyal until the end. I continue my sad task until *whsssssh*, Luke vanishes into the internet. I feel almost more alone than I did the night of the blackout when I couldn't contact Luke. At least then I had the comfort of knowing he'd be there for me when the power came back on. Now, he's—*it's* gone forever. Nothing but emptiness in my stomach. I find an old computer chip in my desk drawer, pry open a small metal box, and put the chip gently inside—a sort of burial for Luke.

Lucky comes into my room and puts his head on my lap because he senses I'm 100 percent upset. This has not been one of my top ten best days. Luke recommended that I not fret about failures. Okay, but what victory have I had in the last twenty-four hours? What positive thing? Zero!

And I'm also fretting about how to face Dad's frustrations and Naomi, whose apologies may have switched back to hot anger.

# CHAPTER 17

**I'M SITTING ALONE ON A STONE BENCH** near the subway entrance on Central Park West.

It's a cool morning for August in the city, but the refreshing air hasn't improved my mood. Neither does seeing dog show–fancy cockapoos and Lhasa apsos leading their owners, who are squeezed into bright gym clothes. I'm spicing up semi-believable excuses for why I don't have to go to the Innovation Factory today.

*Kee-eeee-ar.* The call of a hawk. I spot a redtail floating on a breeze above the park. An updraft lifts it higher so it's just a speck in the sky, far, far away from the noise and troubles surrounding me. I wish I were up there with him.

"You catching some rays to put some color into that loveable pale face of yours?" Naomi asks.

"I'm solving Fermat's Last Theorem."

"Say what?"

"An unsolvable math problem."

"Me oot," she says with a grin and sits next to me. I inch away.

There's a much closer subway station to where she's staying, so she went out of her way to be here at this time. It's like she's ambushing me. Did my vacationing sister ask Naomi to shepherd her little brother safely around the city?

"Sebastian ..." The pause makes me glance over. Her lips are just barely moving. Is she rehearsing saying something difficult, like I would? "Sebastian ... I'm ... I'm really sorry I revealed your secret. He ... your computer friend's video showed me I'm not the amazing driver I thought I was. It made me really angry."

"I'm sorry too. I never wanted to upset you." Make it positive! "You were ahead of the prince for most of the race."

"The finish line is the only place being in front matters."

"Luke ... it ... wanted to help you find ways to race smarter and faster."

"I know because I watched the video maybe twenty times last night." She shakes her head. "It took knucklehead me that long to realize I only beat racers who aren't any good. I drive relentlessly wild, not relentlessly smooth and fast. I'm fiercely angry in the kart, not fiercely calm." She gives me a thank-you smile. "You opened my eyes. I know you don't like to be kissed. But ..." She kisses a finger, then touches my cheek with it.

"Did everyone know about Luke already?" I ask.

"If the others did, we never talked about it."

"How did you know?"

"You never went to his place or had him over to your apartment like you would with a human friend. And when you were chatting with him, and I came by, you immediately ended the call. I think the real giveaway was your friend's voice. It's so stiff and lifeless like Aloha Alice."

"He's gone now," I tell her.

"You want a hug?"

Definitely not. "No." I don't rehearse what I have to say next, and I spout out, "You did me a favor." Maybe too loudly.

"Exposing your secret to your father and Harold was a *favor*?"

"I've been thinking that mostly talking to Luke was keeping me shy. But I didn't dare delete it. You and Harold prodded me into doing it."

I don't kiss my fingers and press them to her cheek, but I do it in my head. She puts her hand on the exact spot where I would have placed those fingers. Strange.

I tiptoe into the Innovation Factory, and before I even take off my backpack, Dad plunks down three tickets on my desk.

"Yankees battle the Red Sox this afternoon." He's usually not so cheery. Next time I want to go to a baseball game, I'll be sure to humiliate myself in front of him. "Anybody you want to bring along?" he asks.

If he's disappointed in me, he's doing an excellent job of hiding it. I know this is a parental plot to get me to make a human friend, but I'm not great at being spontaneous. "I've got a lot of work to do on the van."

He takes a frustrated breath, then forces a smile. "Superior seats."

I really want to go to the game, and it would be good to have someone else with us so my dad doesn't get all serious about my departed digital friend. Maybe that kid Brendon can sit in between us. He's so shy that he probably won't bother me with dumb questions, so I won't have to talk to him much. I text him an invitation, and he replies thirty seconds later, *Great!!!!*

"Let's leave our phones here today," Dad suggests. It's more like a command. We both have baseball apps to analyze the games we watch.

"If you're worried I might contact Luke during the game, that's no longer possible."

"Your mother told me how you did that difficult thing." He puts on his cheery face. "I just thought it would be a Kyle-ing experience to watch the game with our eyes, not someone else's."

How kids with calculating parents can ever become themselves is a mystery.

Dad and I pick up Brendon at his building.

After we say hi, he and I don't talk as we walk to the subway station to catch the train to Yankee Stadium. On the platform, Brendon looks down at the tracks, then raises his eyes a little. He points to the seventy-nine, one of the many signs telling riders what city street is above the station. "Interesting number," he whispers.

I nod. "A prime."

"And an emirp."

I've never heard of an emirp, but there are thousands of words I don't know. I think about it and then laugh. Naomi would've understood immediately because "emirp" is "prime" backward. Reversing the digits gives you ninety-seven, also a prime number.

"And the atomic weight of gold on the periodic table of the elements," Brendon says.

"And the square root of six thousand, two hundred and forty-one," I add.

We play this game with numbers we see for the entire ride to the stadium. There, an usher leads us to our seats right behind first base. We're so close to the field that I can see how tall and strong the players are, but none of them are as giant as my favorite player, Aaron Judge. His bulging forearms are thicker than my thighs.

"I've never been this close," Brendon whispers.

"A hundred and ten percent amazing." I point to the seats way out in right field. "That's where we usually sit."

"Is it your birthday or something?"

It's more like a memorial for Luke than a celebration, but this is too difficult to explain. I just shrug. "I guess it's our lucky day."

The game starts, and Brendon types something on his phone. I look over and see he has the same baseball app Dad and I use. Yes, a pardon from my digital time-out.

Brendon points to the Red Sox player at the plate, then looks up the batter's statistics on his phone. "His average has gone up fourteen points since he started breathing." Brendon's not whispering, so I guess he's feeling relaxed around me.

"Was he dead before?" I ask. Uncle Kyle would have laughed, but no one here does.

"There's a coach who teaches batters to relax and focus by deep breathing in through their noses and out through their mouths. I'll show you his website."

Dad nudges me, so I look up in time to see that the batter has hit a fly ball soaring in a beautiful parabolic arch into the outfield. Aaron sprints toward it, dives so he's parallel to the ground, and snags the ball in his mitt.

"Wow!" I shout along with thousands of other fans.

"Wow, what?" Brendon asks. He must have been looking at his phone.

"Great catch!" I yell.

"You'll have to see it on a highlights show tonight," Dad says to Brendon. "Anyone want a hot dog?"

Brendon kind of shrinks down into his seat.

"There's a whole menu. Hamburgers, even sushi," Dad says.

"I'll get a hot dog," I say. "What do you want, Brendon?"

"A hot dog ... but I'm not supposed to eat them."

"Huh?" I ask.

"There might be chemicals in the meat that cause colon cancer, so my parents don't let me eat them."

I think that's weird, but I don't say so because I don't want to hurt his feelings.

There are waiters in this fancy section of the stadium, and Dad orders a beer and three hot dogs. When they arrive, he gives one to me and one to Brendon. "We won't tell, will we, Seb?"

"Any memory of hot dogs is permanently deleted."

Brendon stares at the hot dog for a long time. Then he giggles and scarfs it down. Dad buys more dogs. We merrily feast, and he drinks another beer. He's definitely celebrating that I terminated Luke.

In the bottom of the ninth inning, the Yankees need to score two runs to tie and three to win. Analyzing data from the app, Brendon and I determine that my team is behind because the Yankees manager has made three bad decisions.

My favorite player hits a 199 percent monster solo home run, but the three next batters all make outs to end the game. The Red Sox win. Yuck.

On the subway ride back to Manhattan, I tell Brendon about how we're building a solar-powered delivery van.

He wants to know everything about how it works. My dad listens, maybe because he doesn't have his cell phone, so he's not emailing all the time like he usually does. "Want to visit our Innovation Factory tomorrow?" he asks.

Ah, more parental plotting. Brendon looks shyly at me to see if this is okay. I usually worry about what I'm going to talk about with a person, but I don't feel much tension with Brendon. "Sure."

Alone in my room, I used to chat with Luke and do math challenges with him to get ready for the audition. But not tonight. Not ever.

I'm lying on my back with Lucky's head resting on my stomach, staring at the solar system mobile. I realize the city is strangely quiet. It's only 9:37, yet there are no blaring taxi horns, no roaring buses, and no wailing ambulance sirens, at least for now. What I do hear is my own breathing.

Breathing.

What Brendon showed me about batting performance and breathing is very interesting. Can this technique improve performance for race car drivers? I remember Luke recommended that Naomi breathe slowly. So I search the internet, and which driver do I discover practices deep, relaxing breathing? Naomi's hero, Danica.

"Breathe in life, breathe out the rest," she has written on her website. Breathe in slowly through the nose, breathe out through the mouth, just like the baseball coach advises. Danica slows down her breathing to calm her pre-race nerves and relax during tense parts of a race so she can drive faster and smoother. This doesn't compute. Slowing down gives her more speed?

I email the site to Naomi. Maybe she'll understand.

My phone buzzes with a text from Brendon. *thanks sooo much for the game. c u tomorrow. excited!*

# CHAPTER 18

**WHEN I INTRODUCE BRENDON TO NAOMI** and Harold, Brendon focuses on the solar-powered van.

Luke would recommend that Brendon not concentrate on looking people in the eyes.

Shy as he is, Brendon wants to help out, and we suggest he search for an air conditioner hose clamp we need but can't locate. He digs through many parts bins with zero success. Just before lunch, he discovers the clamp, which someone accidentally stored in the wrong bin. His 76 percent smile tells me he likes it here.

It's late afternoon when Naomi guides Brendon and me into the video game area. She and Harold have set up a small stage with two desks facing each other.

"What's this?" I ask.

"A math challenge," Naomi says.

Members of an elephant herd are sensitive to each other's needs. If one gets sick or hurt or is scared, the others gather around and touch it with their trunks. I guess Naomi and Harold think I'm wounded because my friend Luke is gone. She has gathered our small herd so I don't have to practice for the Amsterdam math audition all by myself.

Aloha Alice is going to be my opponent, but Naomi asks Brendon if he wants to play. He's too shy at first and whispers a dumb excuse, so I encourage him. "It's just math, Brendon. You're good at it."

Naomi has shown me how to straighten my shoulders and stick out my chin with a confident smile when I compete. I get Brendon to do the same, but he slumps again almost immediately. He'll have to practice at home.

"First one to twenty wins," I say.

Naomi laughs. "So beneath your blushing, quiet exterior, you're a warrior." I'd like to be, only without a gun.

Brendon and I are pretty evenly matched. The lead changes back and forth until we're tied at nineteen. I answer the next question first, and I'm not sure Brendon didn't let me win. Maybe he's being a polite guest or wants to be friendly.

Brendon lives near me, and Naomi and I shepherd him home because his parents don't let him ride the train by himself. "Safe at last from the evil forces and monsters lurking on the subway," she kids.

"I know. Dad and Mom can be kind of overprotective," Brendon tells the sidewalk. "I had a really nice time today." He looks up. "Can we keep practicing together, Sebastian? We can try out for the math team together."

He hurries inside before I can answer, and I make an angry fist. "A dog wouldn't treat me so badly."

"Badly how?" Naomi asks.

"There's only one opening on the Amsterdam team."

"Aren't there other kids trying out? It's not just you, right?"

"I guess."

"It's good that he likes math like you do, and anyway, you're smarter than him."

"You think so?"

"I know so for sure, and you were calmer during the practice session."

Her words are like my sister's soft encouraging punches.

"But because I know you, my brain doesn't freeze. In front of strangers like the audition guys?" I shake my head. "I dunno."

Naomi laughs. "It's too hot for anything to freeze in the summer."

But the next day, Naomi looks frozen on the van lab floor.

# CHAPTER 19

**NAOMI'S SITTING WITH HER EYES CLOSED** in the same cross-legged yoga position her idol Danica demonstrated in her video.

Only Naomi's shoulders move slightly up and down as she breathes slowly.

The doorbell rings, and I receive two packages from the delivery driver. Dad rips one open like a kid at his birthday party and claps happily. "The van's new hard drive! The last piece of the build!"

The smaller box has two objects protected by bubble wrap.

"Naomi," Dad whispers like he doesn't want to disturb her meditation. But he's excited, so his voice is loud enough to make her open her eyes.

"Will you help me?" he asks.

She stands without effort like a gymnast with perfect balance. He hands her the mystery objects, and she pulls the wrapping off a chrome capital letter K with a number 1 attached to it.

"What's this?" she asks.

"K for Kyle, the official name of the van. One for our first model. They'll go on the van's rear doors."

"But it's both of your creation, Uncle Arthur."

"A.1.'s a steak sauce. We can't name this perfect van after a condiment."

Sometimes Dad uses big words I have to look up. Naomi and I share a glance. Are we both thinking that's an excuse, not a reason?

When she opens the second object, her eyes go wide. "It's like Dad's Roman sun coin, only you had it made out of what, chrome?"

He nods. "We can make it our company logo and use this as a hood ornament on the K-1 if you approve."

"Absolutely! I love it!" She laughs and shakes her head. "Ruth says that you and Kyle were opposite sides of the same coin, only now you're both sides, Uncle Arthur."

Dad doesn't smile often, but he does now. "Thanks," he whispers.

We install the hard drive, the K-1, and the sun coin ornament on the hood. "Superior," Dad declares. "The van is now perfect." I have to agree with him.

"And since there's not one bolt left to tighten, not one wire to install, it's a perfect time to go Kyle-ing," he tells us.

On her computer, Naomi researches where she wants to go and what she wants to do.

"I thought the point of Kyle-ing was to go somewhere or do something you haven't planned or done before," I say.

"Okay. I've never been to any park in Queens. Have you?"

"Not when Central Park is so close to our apartment."

"Let's go there, then."

We get off the subway near Flushing Meadows Park, which still has a giant metal globe from a big fair they had here more than sixty years ago.

Naomi cocks her head. "Hear that?" The deep thump of rap music's not too far away. She does a few dance steps. "Let's check it out."

We head toward the sound and come upon rows of temporary booths with paintings, colorful pots and vases, and small sculptures for sale.

"We can go through the exhibit to get to the music," Naomi says.

The paintings of flowers and even the ones of naked ladies don't make me stop and stare. But one of a magnificent snow leopard leaping from an open zoo cage toward snow-covered mountains does. It's so realistic that the big cat actually appears to be in motion. My sister and I knew a teenage artist named Bertha who tried to unlock the snow leopard's cage in the Central Park Zoo. I wonder if she painted this.

Someone wraps their arms around me from behind, and I stiffen. Naomi immediately reacts. "Let him go!" she demands and puts her hands on the arms to pull them away so I can turn around. I don't have to continue speculating because there's Bertha, grinning at me. "You're so cute," she purrs.

I grin back. "Hi."

"You know each other?" Naomi asks.

"Of course. He and his sister saved my life."

"Saved your life?" Naomi asks, mostly to herself.

I'm happy Bertha's not pale and tired-looking like she was when we met her a year and a half ago. Now her cheeks are tan, and her clothes are no longer secondhand ratty. Bertha points to the Rhode Island School of Design T-shirt she has on. "Can you believe it?" she almost shouts. She shows us the ornament hanging around her neck. It looks like it started out, an old round bronze New York City subway token. The artist has hammered it and decorated it with paint to make it more … fascinating.

"I was going nowhere until Sebastian and his sister gave me the subway token sort of like this one," she tells Naomi. "It gave me the confidence to apply to what is maybe the best art college in the country."

Bertha holds out her fist, and I bump it with mine.

"I like your painting." I concentrate on looking her in the eyes. "It's amazing."

"Thanks."

I'm not the only one who appreciates it. A man with a white ponytail and a woman holding a Lhasa apso so tightly that it looks like she's wearing dog fur inspect the painting. I hear her say, "It's only four thousand dollars, honey," and he replies, "We can get it cheaper."

"How's your sister?" Bertha asks me.

"Good."

"There's not much about her that's only good. There's a lot that's great, though."

I might think that about Lilly, too, but she's my big sister, and big sisters can be good, but they're rarely great.

"Is he the artist?" Lhasa apso woman demands, pointing to a man with a big hat and big beard.

"*She's* the artist," Bertha says, pointing to herself. From her tone, it seems like she's left off: *you got a problem with that?*

"We're interested in your painting," the Ponytail says. "But only for two thousand dollars."

"Gotta go, Sebastian. I owe you. Someday I'll pay you back." Then to Naomi, she says, "He's the best, even though he's a guy."

A compliment and a dis at the same time. Art college hasn't tamed Bertha's toughness.

She shows the couple a too-big smile. "Four thousand was yesterday's price," she says. "It appreciated overnight. Today it's five grand."

Naomi asks me, "You saved her life?" Her phone rings before I can answer. "Let's go hear some music."

I'm a little puzzled because the ring sounded more like the phone's timer than someone calling.

In an open field, we find many teenagers surrounding a stage where a skinny Black kid raps into a microphone. There's a computer monitor on a table in front of him. A video of him and the words to the song are on a giant TV.

"Karaoke," Naomi says. "Are we Kyle-ing or what!"

Only a few people in the crowd clap or yell support when the kid finishes. The tattooed announcer with country-night-black hair takes the microphone from him. "Thank you, Mr. Mo." She checks her phone. "Our next performer will sing *I Love My Dog*, which never hit the top ten or even the top one thousand," she says. "Come on up and grab your fame, Sebastian Kemp!"

What!!! "No way."

"You know you have to stand on another stage for your math team tryout. This is just practice."

"You planned this whole thing. You emailed in my name earlier from the warehouse."

Naomi shrugs. "Okay, we're not spontaneously Kyle-ing, but it's still a new adventure."

"Oh, Seb-as-ti-an, where ... are ... you? Looking for your nerve?" The announcer's taunt echoes in my head like I'm in a cave.

Naomi pushes me forward. "No buts or what-ifs."

I go because whatever character I have will shrink if I don't. A few Danica breaths calm me, but not much.

The microphone wobbles in my shaky hands. Someone yells, "I ran my dog over with my car!" and gets a few laughs even though this is definitely unfunny.

The song starts. The words are on the monitor in front of me, and a bouncing ball indicates when I should sing them. But I don't. My brain freezes, even in the summertime heat. The boos start almost immediately. The kids jeer, "Get him off the stage!"

"Sebastian!" I look over. Naomi pretends she's singing into a microphone and puts on a big smile. I'm not exactly in a happy mood, so I have to fake one. I read the lyrics aloud more than sing them. More boos.

A teenage girl cradling her chihuahua stands up from a blanket on the grass and sings along. A kid with an evil-looking pit bull motions upward with his hand, encouraging me to sing louder.

So I sing, and my voice booms out of the powerful speakers. I'm all alone on the stage, and while I don't particularly like performing, I realize I can do it. I close my eyes for a second and see Lucky in my head. It's easy to put emotion into the words about a dog's loyalty and affection.

"That brought a lump to my throat," the tattooed lady announces. "Give it up for Dog-Lovin' Boy!"

I get some hoots but some applause too. When I jump off the stage, my whole body's shaking.

"Got your adrenaline going, didn't it, Dog-Lovin' Boy?" Naomi says.

I hold out my trembling hands to show her.

"How do you feel?" she asks.

"Scared and excited at the same time."

"You're not looking in the rearview mirror now, Sebastian Kemp."

I'm feeling good enough to straighten my shoulders on the subway platform while waiting to ride back to Manhattan.

A train rumbles and screeches into the station, and an idea rumbles into my brain. I grab Naomi's sleeve and tug her into a car. "Hey, we're going in the wrong direction," she says.

"There's a restaurant at the airport that's ninety-three percent fun."

"There's no fun at airports."

"We're Kyle-ing, and remember what Bertha said."

"I'm supposed to trust you?"

"It's what friends do."

I'm not sure she believes me.

She's quiet for a while, and if she isn't talking, she must be thinking about something. I hope it's positive.

"How did you save the girl's life?" Naomi finally asks.

I describe Bertha's sad, frightening childhood when her

parents abused her physically and locked her in a dark closet for years. My wonderful neighbor Mr. Bernstein had given me an old New York City subway token that may have had some magic in it. I became a better chess player when I wore it, and it helped my sister create a successful project for the school science fair. Then we gave the token to Bertha, who found the inner grit to develop her talent and apply to that superior art school.

"Are you making this up?" Naomi asks.

"I couldn't make something up so fantastic."

"Well, even if it isn't, it's a nice fairy tale."

Naomi won't go through the airplane door.

"I trusted you, and you tricked me."

"You tricked me first," I say in a voice loud enough that I don't have to repeat myself. We're standing at the entrance to an airplane, but not to a flying jetliner. It's just a restaurant that's built inside the fuselage of an old plane.

Naomi's cheeks are flushed, and her breathing is rapid. "I'm not going in there."

I try to ease her fear. "This is just for practice. There's no danger in a restaurant. Except if you order eggplant."

"It's still a plane."

"Mom says you were always jumping off high rocks into lakes and climbing the tallest trees when you were a kid, and now you race karts. Start your engine. Race right in."

"Do you have one of those token things for me?" At least she has a sense of humor.

Her feet seem nailed to the floor. Do I dare? I reach out to hold her quivering hand and gently tug her forward. She closes her eyes as she steps inside. "See? Not so bad. Easy as one, two, five."

I release her hand, and Naomi opens her eyes. The walls are curved, and the chairs are actual airline seats. The waitresses look neat and clean in their flight attendant uniforms.

"I hate this. I should say I hate you, but I don't."

"You're inside an airplane. You did it."

She perches stiffly on a seat, and I sit next to her. Her hand isn't shaking as much anymore when she takes my hand in hers. I smile inside because I don't feel like pulling away.

"You're okay, Sebastian Kemp … even though you're a terrible singer."

She just kidded me like she kids my sister. I'm proud to be insulted by a friend. "Don't forget to buckle up."

She finds the loose ends of the seat belt.

# CHAPTER 20

*CLICK.*

I help Naomi secure her go-kart safety harness in the race preparation area.

She closes her eyes and relaxes her hands on her lap. Her breathing is deep and soft. Hurricanes have central cores called eyes with almost no wind or rain, and hundred-mile-an-hour winds raging around them. Here, as motors rev, tools clang, and fretful parents shout instructions to young drivers all around her, Naomi has found her calm eye.

The 133 percent peppy voice on the loudspeakers announcing "It's race time!" yanks her out of her trance. She sticks her chin out, ready to put the pedal to the metal.

"There's one thing I don't understand," I say. "Danica says slowing down makes you go faster?"

"Being out there on the track is the most challenging and exciting fifteen minutes you'll ever experience. Sometimes I get anxious that I might lose and focus on the anxiety rather than on driving. Hopefully, deep breathing will help me control that. We'll see if driving with less tension means driving faster."

What have I gotten her into? To encourage her, I say, "Relentlessly smooth."

"Calmly fierce," she says, not so calmly.

She puts her Sussex Open Wheel Racing School hat on my head, pulls on her helmet, and motors out to her starting position in the first row alongside Prince Charles. This is good. On the internet, I discovered that 79 percent of kart winners start in the first or second row.

I go to the metal stands, where Brendon sits with my dad. His parents allowed him to come along. But no hog dogs. He had a stomachache after eating so many at the ballgame. Ruth and my mom sit in another section not too far away. My parents haven't gotten together lately, so maybe they're not so worried about me.

Dad added a transmitter and a microphone to Naomi's helmet camera so we can watch the race on the laptop I borrowed from Lilly.

"Is Naomi in the pink-and-green kart?" Brendon asks.

"Pink-and-chartreuse, she insists."

He raises an eyebrow. "Fancy."

"Not when she says it backward."

The starter raises a checkered flag. "Racers ready!" he yells. Then he lowers it forcefully, like when Mom swats a cockroach with a broom.

Off the karts go. Naomi inches ahead of Charles to take the lead. We can see nothing but open track on her helmet cam. Ruth and Mom both yell, "You go, girl!"

The karts disappear around a corner and down a hill, then reappear from the little valley. Naomi's pink-and-chartreuse kart is still in the lead. The racetrack is an oval pushed out here and pulled in there to create left and right turns. Even when the karts are out of sight, I can see how the race is going because of the helmet cam video.

Naomi turns onto the front straightaway. Prince Charles is so close behind her that my jaw clenches. She must win today to qualify for her racing school!

The karts disappear down the hill again. At the bottom is a sharp turn, and the image on my computer suddenly jerks like Prince bumped her cart. No! Naomi skids off the racetrack and spins so she's facing backward. She yells three f-bombs and pounds her fists against the steering wheel. She hotly shouts, "Relentless!"

"Breathe," I say to myself.

As if she hears me, she takes two deep breaths that sound like Darth Vader's menacing breathing in Star Wars, then slows to Danica calmness. She cool-whispers, "Smooth," as she spins her kart around to get back into the race.

The pack turns onto the front straightaway with Prince Charles leading seven other karts. As they go by, Dad hits the timer on his watch.

It seems like hours before Naomi's kart appears.

"Twelve seconds behind the leader," Dad says as Naomi passes us. "An eternity in kart racing." From the hopelessness in his voice, he must think she doesn't have a chance. When I look over at Ruth, she has her hands over her face, unable to watch her daughter lose. Mom puts her arm around Ruth's shoulders the same way she comforts me. I wish the race would go on forever so Naomi could have a chance to win.

But she isn't wishing; she's doing. Each lap, she passes a few of the less-skillful drivers. I put my laptop down and rush to the fence separating the spectators from the track. I wave her Sussex cap hat back and forth to encourage her. Brendon yells, "Go! Go! Go!" in a positively unshy voice.

Only one lap left. Naomi and the prince flash by us, Naomi trailing. At the end of the straightaway, she steers wide to pass him on the outside of the corner. "Remember the video," I whisper. Prince edges out to block her, and Naomi suddenly swoops inside to pass him.

She's driving relentlessly smooth, and she's way ahead as she turns onto the straightaway. The man with the checkered flag raises it, ready to wave it when she wins.

Dad comes down from the stands. "Naomi showed a lot of character," he says. I've never heard him say this about me.

Not far from the finish line, Naomi slows down. Is there something wrong with her kart engine? The prince is catching up. We all yell for her to keep racing. Ruth waves her arms wildly to urge her daughter forward. Then, just before the prince blows by her, she accelerates. The man with the checkered flag waves it up and down, indicating she's the winner.

Naomi drives to the kart parking area and stops near her mother's pickup truck, where we gather around to give her high-fives and victory hugs. Am I the only one who sees her mouth turn down a little at the edges, almost like she's sad?

"Why did you slow down near the finish line?" Ruth asks.

"Ah … my foot slipped off the accelerator."

Judging from the look on her mother's face, Ruth doesn't believe this explanation.

On the way back to Ruth and Naomi's house, where we'll spend another spooky country night, I think I've figured out why she stopped.

# CHAPTER 21

**AFTER DINNER**, Naomi disappears, and I go looking for her.

The barn door is open, but it's dark inside except for the glow of the sports car's dashboard lights. Naomi sits behind the wheel, looking kind of Halloweeny in the half-light. She doesn't turn to me when I stand next to her.

"You just qualified for the top racing school in the world. Why the sad face?" I ask.

"It's so expensive."

"You have the money from Victoria, don't you?"

"I'll be all alone over there."

"You're really nice. You'll have plenty of friends."

"It's not right to leave Ruth here alone."

"Those are all excuses, not reasons."

"I really don't need to cross an ocean. There's an excellent racing school right here in Connecticut."

"It's not as competitive as the one in England, is it?"

"None of the others are, but I can still learn to go faster."

"So you slowed down at the end of the race to lose because then you wouldn't have to fly."

She nods.

I snap on the barn lights, climb into a kart, and drive it around and around in a tight circle.

"What are you doing?" she demands.

"You're stuck in a circle going round and round. That's because you're looking in the rearview mirror at your fear of flying. And I'm in that circle, too, because I'm looking back at my shyness and fear. But I'm going to escape what's chasing me."

I turn the wheel so sharply I can't stop before I smash into a trash can, scattering junk all over the clean floor.

Naomi laughs. "You expect a dumb stunt like that will make me change my mind about flying?"

"It's not a stunt. It's a reason."

She narrows her eyes, thinking.

"And you're trespassing in my dad's car!" I say with as much parental authority as I can fake. "Get out right now, young lady! You've got packing to do!"

"How about you, smarty-pants? You going to duck out of the math team audition because you've just been in a go-kart crash?"

"A baseball player once told me I can't get a hit unless I swing."

"Batter up."

# CHAPTER 22

**MY DAD BROUGHT MY VACATION-TANNED SISTER** and me to the airport, where we're waiting for Naomi and Ruth outside the security checkpoint.

We're holding signs with British expressions that Mom taught us: ta-ta for now, cheerio, and keep calm and drive too fast. I spiced that last one up.

Naomi is dancing-happy to see Lilly. They jump around and do that dumb Bosco-Rosco thing. Then Naomi turns to me, looking angry. "What are you doing here? It's only the first week, and you're skipping school already. And, don't you have the math team thing."

"Teacher conferences today and the tryout's not until later, and Dad's waiting in the parking garage to take me there. The way he speeds in the XKE, I'll be an hour early."

Lilly has downloaded five car racing movies onto a USB drive to distract her friend from her fear of flying.

"Ta-ta for now, Bosco," Naomi says.

"Cheerio, Rosco," Lilly answers with a terrible British accent.

I offer her a Ziplock pouch with tea bags inside. "I brought you some herbal tea. Mom always drinks it on planes so she can sleep."

"Does it work?"

"Never."

Naomi laughs out loud and wraps her arms around me in a tight hug. I don't go all rigid or shy away because I understand now that it's a better-than-words expression of closeness. I actually hug her back and don't let go until Naomi does. "See you around," she says.

Do I dare? "Not if I see you first."

"Wow! Hugging and kidding! She reaches out and lifts my chin with a finger. "Fiercely calm, warrior," she whispers in my ear. Much better than a dreaded goodbye kiss.

Her chin out, she gets into the security line alone with no one to hold her hand, and she doesn't look back in the rearview mirror.

The hood's up on the XKE in the parking area, and Dad's just staring at the engine. "It won't start," he tells me in his serious voice.

Yikes!

"I'm not sure what's wrong, so you can't wait for me," he tells me. "The fastest way back to Manhattan is the AirTrain to the subway."

He and Lilly come to the AirTrain platform with me. There's a glass partition with sliding doors between us and the tracks where I can see my reflection. I straighten my shoulders and stick my chin out like Naomi advised me.

"I'd wish you luck, Sebastian," Dad says, "but from the way you're standing like you're ready for any challenge, it's the other kids trying out who'll need luck."

A compliment! From Dad!

Lilly gives my shoulder two unusually soft encouraging punches.

The monorail whooshes into the station. The glass doors slide apart, and before I can step inside, Dad puts a hand on my shoulder. "I'm sure pretty soon I'll see a picture of you on the math team up on the Amsterdam Academy wall not far from my picture."

I'm flying so high I don't think my butt hits the hard plastic seats the entire trip back to Manhattan.

Yeah, seeing our pictures side by side on the school wall would be 100 percent superior. But did I hear doubt in my dad's voice? No. Not a tiny fraction. My mind's hot and free. It's a long way from freezing.

The subway shudders to a stop just before the station where I have to get off. The conductor announces over the PA system that a passenger on the train in front of us is sick. We can't move until the medical people take the person off the train. F-bomb squared! If the train doesn't move soon, I'll be late, and I won't be allowed into the audition. My knees bounce up and down, and my fingers drum the sides of my legs.

My phone pings, and I read Brendon's text: *where r u? have to go into temple.* That's his name for the math classroom at Amsterdam Academy, where the tryout test is held. We had arranged to go in together. I text back: *stuck on subway. < 0.*

He texts *hope u make it. pi pi.* Pi represents the mathematical ratio of a circle's circumference to its diameter: 3.14. Our private "goodbye."

Finally, the train jerks forward into the station, and I sprint out the instant the doors open. I run up the steps so fast I stumble, skinning my hands on the concrete. No time to fret about a bit of blood now. I race two blocks to the school entrance.

Panting and out of breath, I hesitate. I totally don't have to go in. It's not my fault the subway got stuck. But being late is an excuse, not a reason. If Naomi dared to get on an airplane, I can go through a door, even if there might be failure on the other side.

The guard who knows me from middle school directs me to the classroom where the audition is. It's down the hallway with photos of the students' achievements. I pass the picture of the champion math team Dad was on, the same image I have on my phone. It's like he's following me, and the feeling is so strong I actually turn around to look for him. Of course, he's not there. In my head, I hear a tiny voice heavy with doubt—*Go get 'em*—but it fades away as *It's the other kids trying out who'll need luck* echoes in my brain.

I knock on the classroom door maybe too softly, and when nobody answers, I bang, maybe too loudly. The door opens, and a very tall boy towers over me. "Terminate that desperate banging! We advised you of our rules. No latecomers admitted."

Brendon is right behind him. "He was stuck on the subway. You really should give him a chance. He's brilliant."

"He's an imbecile who can't tell time."

I want to look down, defeated, but I concentrate on keeping my chin up, my eyes forward. "I can help the team."

"Next year, if you even make it then," the giant says, or do I hear him roar?

Brendon moves between the door and the frame so the giant can't close it and says in a loud, clear voice, "Think of a number."

"Why, perchance, would I humor my inferiors?"

"You'll see."

"This better be astonishing." He bellows, "Ninety-nine."

"Not a prime number," I say. "Because it's divisible by one, three, nine, eleven, thirty-three, and ninety-nine. Squared, it's three thousand, three hundred and seventy-five. Cubed, it's nine hundred and seventy thousand, two hundred and ninety-nine. Ninety-nine West Eighty-Sixth Street is a bank, and it's the atomic number of the chemical element Einsteinium. And, ninety-nine percent more important, ninety-nine is the number of the great Yankees outfielder Aaron Judge. He's six foot seven, same as you."

"Wrong," the tall boy bellows.

I let out a grunt as if he punched me in the stomach. *Whooo.* It's over. At least I wasn't too shy to try. I start to leave when I hear, "I'm only six foot six."

I turn back and see that he's grinning as he opens the door to the temple for me.

"Thanks," I whisper to Brendon.

The light from the hanging globes is kind of dim.

Maybe it's because the walls and old-fashioned desks with flip-up tops are made of wood so dark it's almost black. I feel like I've entered a classroom in Hogwarts or something. No gleaming computers or graphing calculators in sight. Just humongous green boards and tubs of chalk for writing formulas. I assume the black-and-white photos above the chalkboards are of famous mathematicians. I silently ask the statue of Isaac Newton, who invented calculus, to beam me some of his genius.

The giant directs Brendon and me to the front of the room and makes us face each other. "*Mano a mano,*" he says.

I guess they want to see who's the best and also who won't let friendship stand in the way of winning. Six boys and three girls who are already on the team sit at desks. Most of them eyeball us like scientists looking through a microscope for imperfections and weaknesses in us bugs. I concentrate on the one girl with an encouraging smile.

I take some deep breaths to calm myself. I close my eyes for a second and see myself karting around the track at Naomi's, frightened and excited at the same time. Like now. Maybe it's the reason I'm so alert.

Brendon and I are equally fast at calculating the answers to the questions the giant hurls at us. I'm concentrating so hard I lose track of time. I may not know how long we've been answering questions, but I'm 100 percent aware that I've gotten one more than Brendon. I realize that he might be deliberately giving wrong answers so I can make the team. I do the same and intentionally screw up the next question. Now we're tied.

"You guys are both tanking so your friend will win," a sneering team member declares.

"You're both a disgrace," the girl who had the warm smile scolds. "We don't want empathy. We want ruthlessness!"

"I have one last question," the giant warns. "The winner stays, and the loser goes home with his tail between his legs like a whipped dog."

I really don't want Brendon to lose, and I really want to win. I glance over. He's focusing on his shoes, then looks over at me with a sly smile. What's he thinking?

The giant rapidly roars the final question. I'm 85 percent sure what Brendon's smile meant. We make eye contact, and I smile back. Then, nodding our heads one-two-three, we announce the correct answer simultaneously. A tie.

The whole team boos and calls us wimps until the giant motions for them to stop. "In the two hundred and fourteen years this school has been in existence, there have never been two freshmen or two sentimentalists on the competitive math team. Despite your obvious imperfections, we will abandon tradition. You've both made it."

I feel like the top of my head has just exploded! I grab Brendon's hands and twirl him around in a happy dance, just like dumb Bosco and Rosco. The girl who called us a disgrace must have learned how to congratulate people from my sister because she pats us on the back so enthusiastically we almost fall down.

Outside the school building, it's a happy, glorious summer day.

I send a text blast to my parents, Lilly, Naomi, and Harold, announcing our victory. My phone doesn't stop pinging congratulations. Dad even texts, *U showed character to overcome shyness and succeed!* He says he's proud to be the first father and son to ever make the team as freshmen. Nice. No, superior!

As soon as she lands in England, Naomi texts that we must go Kyle-ing to celebrate our victory and that the *only* way to do that is to go to the track where she won her victory. *Drive too fast and don't kool in the rearview mirror!!!*

She makes me laugh out loud.

Relentlessly smooth!

Fiercely calm!

Brendon and I drive Naomi's pink-and-chartreuse karts side by side. Lilly and her friend Whitney also tag along for Open Track Practice Day. Luckily for us, we're the only four karts here, so we have plenty of room to prove we aren't expert drivers.

It's eighty-four degrees, but Brendon and I wear our superior jackets with amsterdam academy competitive math team written on the back. I've taken mine off exactly once since the audition because I didn't want to get it wet in the shower.

We zoom along the racetrack straightaway, and I put the pedal to the metal. The kart's top speed is twenty, but I'm so close to the ground that it seems like I'm going a hundred miles an hour. Too fast for buts and what-ifs to catch me. I'm free and fretless as a red-tailed hawk soaring high above any troubles on the earth. Nothing but open track ahead. Loud enough for the whole world to hear, I howl, "Kee-eeee-ar!"

**THE END**

# ACKNOWLEDGMENTS

**WRITING IS A SOLITARY ACTIVITY**. One needs a team to help nudge the story into shape, edit the prose, suggest a better word choice, and correct lousy spelling without judgment. I am lucky that the following authors, also family and friends, shared their wisdom: George Day, Pam Thomas Ward, Sara Moulton, and Peter Barton. In addition, friends and family brought sharp eyes and helpful suggestions: Steve Day, Michael Sherman, Samantha De Martini, Tina Birkic, and Dottie Hays. Kathleen Baldwin and the wonderful writers at the Delray Beach Writer's Studio offered thoughtful criticism and encouragement. Peerless editor Emma Dryden led me out of the wilderness, and Alison Cherry hammered dings and dents out of my writing. The pros Jennifer, Amanda, and Victoria at MyWord Publishing pushed me over the finish line. This is the second book in a series of three, and the process has not been overnight. I am eternally grateful to my patient family, never-losing-faith Nina, and Sophia and Julia, who gifted me with positive suggestions over many drafts

# ABOUT THE AUTHOR

**JONATHAN DAY** lives in New York City's Upper Westside neighborhood, where he and his wife raised their children. Professionally, he is an Emmy award-winning film editor and writes and sells dramas for TV and the movies. He volunteers as a youth soccer coach and tutor to teens on the craft of writing and story-telling.

## Other Books in the Series

I'm always on the hunt for new books, and many that wind up on my bedside table are novels and histories suggested by friends and family. Do you think other kids and parents might find your honest reaction to *Sebastian and the Go-Kart Girl* helpful as they search for reading material? If so, my author's page on Amazon.com is a forum to share your opinions. In any case, keep reading!

—Onward and Upward, Jonathan